W9-CAF-066

My Life as a Cartoonist

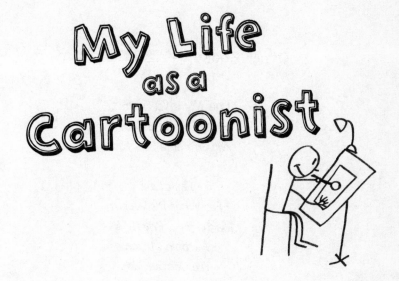

Other Books by Janet Tashjian

Praise for
My Life as a Stuntboy

"Another fun, emotionally resonant read for the Wimpy Kid set and beyond." —*Kirkus Reviews*

"This is a great package for kids, especially those like Derek who don't think they like to read.... The draw of the story is matched by Tashjian's keen observations of how kids really feel and how they interact with the world." —*Booklist*

"A fast-moving plot and relatable protagonist make this stand-alone sequel a good choice for boys who, like Derek, would rather reach for a TV remote or game controller than a book." —*School Library Journal*

"Derek's voice remains dry, witty, and above all, honest, and his efforts to overcome his learning disability will certainly strike a chord with those readers struggling with similar issues and offer insight to their bookish counterparts. Jake Tashjian...provides another slew of wonderfully comic stick figures to populate the margins, mirroring and often elaborating on the text's sly humor. Fans of the first will be utterly delighted by this sequel and anxious to see what Derek will turn up as next." —*Bulletin of the Center for Children's Books*

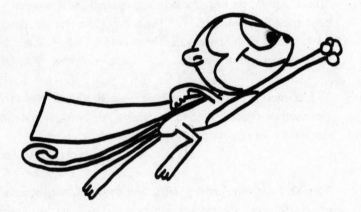

JANET TASHJIAN

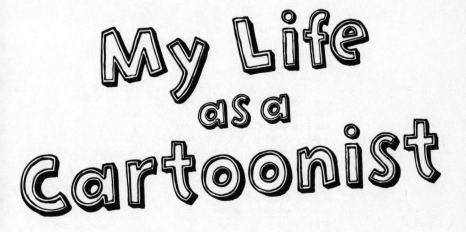

My Life
as a
Cartoonist

with cartoons by
JAKE TASHJIAN

Christy Ottaviano Books
Henry Holt and Company
New York

Henry Holt and Company, LLC
Publishers since 1866
175 Fifth Avenue
New York, New York 10010
mackids.com

Henry Holt® is a registered trademark of
Henry Holt and Company, LLC.
Text copyright © 2013 by Janet Tashjian
Illustrations copyright © 2013 by Jake Tashjian
All rights reserved.

Library of Congress Cataloging-in-Publication Data
Tashjian, Janet.
My life as a cartoonist / Janet Tashjian ; with cartoons by
Jake Tashjian. — First edition.
pages   cm
"Christy Ottaviano books."
Summary: Twelve-year-old Derek wants to train his pet
monkey to help Umberto, a new student who uses a
wheelchair, but Umberto would rather steal Derek's
cartoon ideas.
ISBN 978-0-8050-9609-5 (hardcover) —
ISBN 978-0-8050-9895-2 (e-book)
[1. Cartoonists—Fiction. 2. Wheelchairs—Fiction. 3. People
with disabilities—Fiction. 4. Schools—Fiction. 5. Youths'
art.] I. Tashjian, Jake, illustrator. II. Title.
PZ7.T211135Myc 2013   [Fic]—dc23   2012046201

Henry Holt books may be purchased for business or
promotional use. For information on bulk purchases, please
contact Macmillan Corporate and Premium Sales
Department at (800) 221-7945 x5442 or by e-mail at
specialmarkets@macmillan.com.

First Edition—2013
Printed in the United States of America by R. R. Donnelley & Sons
Company, Harrisonburg, Virginia
10 9 8 7 6 5 4 3 2 1

To Grammy, Oma, and Pop

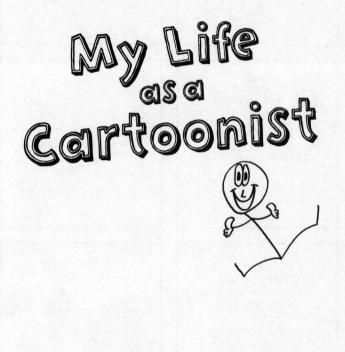

Super Frank!

"That's great!" my dad says as he puts the comic strip down. "Your drawings have really improved."

improved

I look over my father's shoulder and examine my work. "No matter how long I work on it, my printing still looks like I'm in second grade."

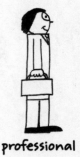

professional

"It takes a lot of practice for lettering to look professional."

As if that's any kid's idea of

fun—sitting around on a sunny afternoon filling notebooks with row after row of straight block letters.

My father closes the cover of the pad and hands it back to me. "Too bad Frank doesn't know he's the star of your comic strip. He'd be flattered."

flattered

Dad doesn't realize I've already shown Frank my drawings. It may be my imagination but by the way my capuchin monkey jumped up and down, I think he WAS flattered.

"Mac and cheese with stewed tomatoes," Mom calls from the kitchen. "Wash up and come to the table."

cringe

My father and I look at each other and cringe. "Why does she take something perfect like macaroni and cheese then throw something terrible like stewed tomatoes in to wreck it?" I ask.

"You know how Mom likes to sneak healthy food into everything," Dad whispers back. "But I have to agree with you—it's a crime to mess with mac and cheese."

As I put away my pad, I realize Dad's inadvertently given me the plot of my next comic strip: SUPER FRANK VS. THE WOMAN WHO WRECKED MAC AND CHEESE.

inadvertently

I can't wait until Ms. McCoddle's class tomorrow to start working on it.

A New Kid in Class

hostages

When I show Matt the new SUPER FRANK, he tells me it's good but needs even more action.

"How about if the evil seal takes hostages at the bank and Super Frank has to break into the building before it blows up?"

If you don't count the seal and the monkey, Matt's suggestion sounds like the plot to a zillion movies we've watched together over the years. But because he's my best friend, I tell him it's a great idea.

"How about if the seal wears a sombrero?" Matt continues. "And one of those long ammunition straps—with scuba gear."

sombrero

I try to envision why a bank robber with a sombrero would need scuba equipment, then take it as a challenge to come up with a scenario where those items actually do make sense.

envision

Matt and I stop in the hall at the same time to continue the discussion. We both act as if the reason we're stopping is because the topic is so important, but our REAL excuse for hitting the pause button is because Carly's at her locker talking to Crash, who's a year

frayed

arrogant

ahead of us. Crash wears his usual school uniform of flip-flops, baggy surf shorts, and a frayed T-shirt. Carly met him at surf camp in Santa Monica a month ago, and lately she's been spending as much time with him as she does with Matt and me.

She waves when she sees us, but Crash doesn't bother to nod even though she's introduced him to us a thousand times.

"He's the most arrogant kid in school," Matt says. "I don't know what she sees in him."

"If he doesn't start combing his hair, he's going to have dreadlocks soon," I add.

"Yeah, because he's not cool enough now," Matt says.

"What's next, a tattoo?"

"He'd be the only person in middle

school with one—if you don't count the teachers." For the past few years, every one of our homeroom teachers has had at least two tattoos.

We immediately drop the conversation when Carly approaches. She's her usual bubbly self, not aware that her two best friends have just been talking about her. "Have you met the new kid?" she asks.

"Your boyfriend, Crash?" I say.

"Crash isn't my boyfriend!" Carly blushes, then gives me a little shove. "Don't you listen to Ms. McCoddle? There's a new kid in our class. He transferred in today."

transferred

Hearing this makes me wonder how much other information I miss when I'm drawing in my notebook during Ms. McCoddle's morning meetings.

"His name's Umberto," Carly says. "I met him a few minutes ago. He's really nice."

"You say that about everyone," I tell her.

"That's not true. Toby is a knucklehead and I'll tell him to his face."

Matt laughs, but I'm surprised by how much more self-assured Carly's become in the last few weeks. Have they started putting something in the Pacific Ocean or is all that fresh air responsible for Carly's shift? Or does Carly's sudden confidence come from hanging around with her buddy Crash?

The bell rings and we head into the classroom. Ms. McCoddle's been on this whole "around the world" decorating theme, so this

confidence

week every inch of the classroom is covered with photographs of Egyptian hieroglyphics as well as the pyramids and the Sphinx. Last month's educational destination was China—I was hoping we'd get some ginger chicken or hot and sour soup along with the photographs, but we didn't get either.

Carly holds out her arms like some woman on TV turning letters on a game show. "Derek, Matt— meet Umberto."

I'm so busy staring at the hieroglyphics above the Smart Board that I almost trip over a kid with a Lakers T-shirt and closely shaved hair. He's parked right between my desk and me, in a wheelchair.

I tell Umberto it's nice to meet

hieroglyphics

PRIVATE

access

him, but before he can answer, Ms. McCoddle asks us to take our seats. Umberto skillfully wheels his chair to a new desk placed next to mine. I've seen a few of these desks in other classrooms—more like a table than a desk—designed for easy access for kids with wheelchairs.

Matt gives me a look that says, "We have a lot to discuss at recess." Our tightly knit class hasn't had a transfer student yet and in all my years of elementary and middle school, I've never sat next to a kid in a wheelchair. As Ms. McCoddle babbles on about the Nile River, I imagine Matt and me on our skateboards, racing down the hill at UCLA alongside Umberto. He's wheeling as fast as he can while Matt and I slalom on either side of him.

As the three of us glide down the hill, I ask Umberto a million questions: What school did he transfer from? Has he always been in a wheelchair? Do his parents have one of those cool vans with a mini elevator?

I snap out of my reverie when Ms. McCoddle pauses at my desk and shoots me the evil eye.

But of all the things I want to talk to Umberto about, the one at the top of my list is this: I HAVE A CAPUCHIN MONKEY WHO'LL SOON BE TRAINED TO HELP PEOPLE IN WHEELCHAIRS!

I can barely contain myself through Ms. McCoddle's lecture on Egyptian artifacts, counting the minutes till I can change Umberto's life with my monkey.

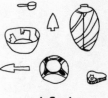

artifacts

A Little Background on Frank

Technically, Frank isn't MY monkey. My parents and I are the foster family he lives with to get used to being with humans. An organization in Boston trains capuchins to work with people with physical challenges and because my mom's a veterinarian—and because I can SOMETIMES be responsible—they chose us as one of the families entrusted with nurturing a monkey.

entrusted

And if you guessed it's my job to change his diapers, you're right.

My friend Michael—who's in a wheelchair like Umberto—lives with a capuchin monkey named Pedro, who helps him with day-to-day living. Michael is seventeen and doesn't mind sometimes hanging out with a twelve-year-old like me—even if he has to because our moms are friends.

Living with Frank has been amazing—if you don't count the time I almost killed him when he swallowed one of my action figures. My dog Bodi was surprisingly welcoming and didn't act jealous at all when Frank moved in. I'm so used to having Bodi's mellow, older energy in the house that Frank's nonstop activity is refreshing.

refreshing

In the six months since we've had Frank, I never thought about who might actually get to live with him after he's been trained. Then out of the blue, the new kid in the very desk next to mine is in a wheelchair and almost crying out for monkey assistance. It's too good to be true, so I immediately do what I ALWAYS do when I'm excited about a new idea. I rummage through my desk for my markers and my trusty pad.

Umberto's not going to believe his luck.

Can Someone Please Tell Me What's Going On?

When the bell rings, I turn to show Umberto my new drawing, but he's already halfway across the classroom, on his way outside to the picnic tables.

"That kid's fast," Matt says.

"I heard he was at his grandma's house in a pretty rough neighborhood and he got shot," Carly whispers. "And THAT'S why he's in a wheel-chair."

"There's no way that happened," I say.

Matt agrees with me. "As if there's someone in our boring middle school in a wheelchair because of a gunfight."

"I'm just saying that's what I heard." Carly runs ahead to Maria and Nancy, already tired of our conversation.

"If it's from a bullet wound—" I begin.

temporary

"It's not," Matt assures me.

"I know, but if it is, do you think the wheelchair is a permanent or temporary thing?"

Matt rolls his eyes. "This is about Frank, isn't it?"

"I'm just saying...if Umberto's in a wheelchair for the rest of his life, someone like Frank could really help him."

Matt looks over my shoulder as I talk; after a few minutes, I turn around to see what he's looking at. Umberto's with three other kids on the edge of the school yard. He has a lacrosse stick in one hand and rapidly spins the wheels of his chair with the other. He leans forward as the ball sails toward him and catches it effortlessly in the basket of the stick.

effortlessly

"He's better at lacrosse than we are," Matt says. "And we can run."

"I don't even know anyone who PLAYS lacrosse," I add. "Where did those guys get sticks?" More important—how does Umberto know so many kids his first week of school?

"I'm not sure he wants to hear about Frank," Matt says.

He's right. Asking Umberto if he

wants to meet my capuchin suddenly seems ridiculous. Crazier still when Umberto skids to a stop in front of me.

"Great catch," I tell him. "Did you play lacrosse at your old school?"

"My old school barely had books, never mind a lacrosse team." Umberto looks over my head as he talks, almost as if he's searching for someone more interesting to talk to.

"So, what happened?" I point to his wheelchair. "Were you in an accident?"

"No, this happened in a chess game," Umberto answers.

breach

I can see Matt start to laugh, then immediately stop, knowing what a breach it would be to side with the new kid over his best friend.

Umberto keeps going. "Maybe YOU were in an accident that left you brain-dead."

"I'm not brain-dead," I say defensively. "Just curious."

"Yeah, like the monkey. I think I'll start calling you George." Umberto pulls up his leather gloves, tightening the small buttons at the top.

"What's your PROBLEM?" I ask. "I was just trying to be friendly."

"Okay, George," he yells over his shoulder as he races away.

I turn to Matt. "Is it me or was he trying to start a fight?"

"Maybe you remind him of somebody he hates," Matt answers.

Great. It's bad enough I had to deal with Joe and Swifty torturing me a few months ago. Now the new kid has me in his sights too.

"Hey, George," Maria says as she, Nancy, and Carly head inside.

"It didn't take Umberto long to get that going," I mumble.

"At least everyone loves Curious George," Carly says.

"When they're in kindergarten," Nancy chimes in.

optimist

Leave it to Carly the optimist— always trying to find the bright side of things. Leave it to almost everyone else in the world to crush my spirit before it's even time for lunch.

As I walk to my seat, I keep my head down. The last thing I'm looking for is trouble, but it finds me anyway.

"Hey, George," Umberto says as he slides behind his desk. "Give my regards to the man in the yellow hat."

This time five or six people hear him and start laughing. I look over at Matt who leans toward my desk.

"You wanted to tell him about

Frank, but Umberto made a monkey
out of you instead."

I pretend like I'm going to laugh,
then shoot Matt a look to shut up.

This is not good. Not good at all.

I Do What I Do Best

When my mother asks me about my day, I tell her about the bolt Stephen DeMarco found in his chili. The lunch ladies insisted the bolt fell out of the fan above the stove and just happened to land in the chili pot, but Matt and I prefer to imagine the lunch ladies are secretly being replaced by robots. Stephen made a big deal over the fact that he could've choked and enjoyed telling the anecdote a dozen more times throughout the day.

anecdote

I DON'T tell my mom that a transfer kid appeared out of nowhere and chose me to turn into his verbal punching bag. I don't tell her because I already know what she'll say. She'll tell me Umberto was probably just nervous because it's his first week at a new school and I should see what he's really like once he settles in. Since I've already had the entire conversation in my head, I spare myself having the real one and just tell her about Stephen's mishap to save myself the trouble.

mishap

Luckily for me, my mom changed Frank's diaper ten minutes before I came home so I'm probably safe for a few hours. (Matt calls it "doodie

perched

duty.") I undo the door of his cage, and Frank immediately runs up my arm. Sometimes my mom carries him around the house in one of those baby carriers, but I like having Frank perched on my shoulder as if we're in the jungle and he just jumped out of a giant palm tree, landing on me to break his fall. I walk through the house looking for Bodi but can't find him anywhere. I grab a few slices of bologna from the fridge and head to the yard to look for him.

Sometimes when it's warm, Bodi likes to lie underneath the jasmine that hangs over the back fence. Sure enough, he's there today, so I split the bologna slices among the three of us and sit down next to him.

It used to be when I skateboarded up the driveway or rode my bike into the yard, Bodi would race over and be there to greet me before I hit the door. These days, he's just happy to see me—at his age he doesn't have the energy for all that running. When I have him out on walks, people who stop to pet him can't believe he's twelve; he still has a lot of bounce for an older dog. I'm probably the only one who notices he gets around slower than before.

When Bodi and I were both younger, I used to love to take him to the dog park, especially when Mr. Danson's greyhound, Murphy, was there. Murphy would lap the park continually, racing like a Thoroughbred, zipping between all the dog owners without ever knocking any

raucous

of them over. Bodi would strain on his leash at the gate if he saw Murphy, then burst into the park and chase him lap after lap until I finally had to drag his tired butt home. I wonder if Bodi ever thinks about those raucous times when he's lying under the jasmine, the way my grandmother remembers all those old stories of taking road trips with her girlfriends even though they're now all seventy years old. I remove Frank from my shoulder and sneak down next to Bodi. The jasmine smells stronger than the bologna, but sweeter, the way I imagine a rain forest would smell.

What was with that kid Umberto today? We could've talked about sports or sneakers or movies but instead he got on the defensive. And why me? Why not Matt or Stephen or Swifty? Was I wearing a sign on my back that said PLEASE BE ABUSIVE? All I can do is hope tomorrow will be different, that Umberto will move onto something—or someone—else.

"Don't tell me that's Frank I see over there. You know he's not supposed to be outside." If there's one thing my mother's good at, it's detecting the smallest infraction when it comes to Frank's routine.

abusive

"He's fine," I yell back. "He's not going anywhere."

infraction

We've had this conversation twelve billion times, but still my mom insists on following the rules from the monkey organization to the letter. No matter where I am, she's ready to jump on the smallest violation. Who can wreck a staring-at-the-clouds,

violation

smelling-jasmine daydream faster than a mom enforcing rules?

I grab Frank, and Bodi dutifully follows us inside. My plan had been to make my mother feel bad for ruining such a great outdoor moment, but when I enter the kitchen, the smell of warm banana bread envelops me like a tropical blanket. When I spot the chocolate glaze she's swirled on top, any thought of giving my mom grief immediately disappears. I even use my best manners so she doesn't complain when I take a second piece.

envelops

I know my reading homework's going to take me all night—a whole chapter!—so I treat myself to a little break before I start illustrating my vocabulary words. Bodi circles the desk in my room, then settles down. He knows the drill. Pad, markers, pen. I was originally going to work on the mac and cheese storyline but I put that idea on the back burner and make some initial sketches of Super Frank in school. Before I know it, I am trying—and failing—to draw a stick figure in a wheelchair.

initial

I rip up the paper and toss it in the trash. Why is this new kid getting under my skin? What's wrong with getting a nickname? Aren't kids SUPPOSED to have nicknames? What's so bad about being curious anyway?

I turn to a fresh white page. But what comes out of my marker this time isn't a stick figure vocabulary word but a sentence. STOP WORRYING.

If I do say so myself, it's pretty good advice.

If my cartoonist career doesn't work out, I can always become a guidance counselor.

guidance

An Embarrassing
Moment

When I get to school the next morning, Umberto's already at his desk. Since I decided yesterday to play it cool, I don't say anything, just go about the business of tossing my books onto the shelf of my chair.

"Hey, George, how's it going?" Umberto asks.

Since my name isn't George, I ignore him.

"You looking to start some trouble, George?"

Umberto may be taller than me when he's standing up but he's not standing up—he's in his wheelchair. I take advantage of this and pull myself up to full height (which admittedly isn't very tall).

"My name's Derek," I answer. "Or should I make up a nickname for you, too?"

sparring

Umberto licks his lips and smiles, as if he's just been waiting for me to engage in this verbal sparring. "You want to give ME a nickname? Like what? Wheelchair boy?"

I am horrified by his sarcasm and can't believe those words just came out of Umberto's mouth. But before I can answer, several of our classmates hover around our desks. Carly looks me in the eye and shakes her head as if to say DO NOT OPEN YOUR MOUTH.

But of course I do. "You're the one who's obsessed with nicknames. Why don't you make up one for yourself?"

Umberto bangs his gloved hands on the armrests of his wheelchair, delighted by the idea. "I AM going to give myself a nickname. How about Derek?" He leans back in his chair and does a series of quick circles in the back of the room. "From now on, everyone should call me Derek!"

Carly shakes her head, which makes me feel even more stupid.

brainiac

"I suppose a brainiac like you would've seen that coming?" I whisper to her after.

"He obviously has it out for you. Just ignore him," she answers.

"It's kind of hard to ignore a new kid popping wheelies in the back of the room and yelling my name." I look over my shoulder to see if Ms. McCoddle's coming to bail me out, but she's still in the hall talking to Mr. Henderson.

"I'm definitely making a comic strip about this," I continue. "I'm going to call it *Wheelchair Bully.*"

scolding

Maria's putting her books away and turns to me with a scolding expression that reminds me of one of my mother's many disapproving faces. "It's not nice to make fun of another kid in our class, especially someone new." She leans over so I can feel her full wrath. "*Especially* someone in a wheelchair."

"ME? I'm the victim, not him."

Just as the words leave my

mouth, I look over Maria's shoulder to see Umberto drop his notebook on the floor. He tries valiantly to pick it up but can't. Three of our classmates race to help him. Stephen reaches it first, brushes it off, and hands it to an apologetic Umberto. This new kid's a better actor than Brad Pitt.

valiantly

apologetic

"Sure, YOU'RE the victim." Maria's look is one of pure disdain. "It's all about you." She turns her back on me in a huff.

"I'm starting to get worried," Carly says.

"You're not the only one."

Since Umberto's changed his name to Derek, maybe my new nickname should be Bullseye.

Dad Gives Me Some Pointers

As soon as I walk in the door, I throw myself into my drawings. Usually, I get impatient trying over and over to capture Frank's various poses, but today I spend hours perfecting just the right position of Frank's arm. When I started immortalizing Frank in my strip, I didn't realize how hard drawing a capuchin monkey would be—much more difficult than the

immortalizing

stick figures I use to illustrate my vocabulary words.

Ms. McCoddle asked me last week if I wanted to enter some of my vocabulary drawings in an exhibit Ms. Myers was putting together in the school library. Part of me was proud she thought my drawings were good enough to put in an exhibit, but another part of me was worried that kids who DIDN'T need help with their reading might make fun of me for still having to illustrate words I don't understand. In the end, I decided not to participate, and I could tell Ms. McCoddle was disappointed. That was before Umberto joined our class; I can only imagine how much grief he'd give me now if I'd joined the exhibition.

What I DID agree to was starting

participate

a cartoon drawing club after school. At first I doubted I had the skills to show other kids how to draw, but Ms. McCoddle convinced me it was a CLUB not a class, and all I'd be doing was sharing my interest in drawing with other like-minded kids. Matt can barely draw a circle but he signed up immediately when I posted the club info on the school website. He also put together an outline for a comedy movie club for the after-school program. I was happy to reciprocate by signing up for his.

reciprocate

"Your technique is really coming along," my father says when he examines my work. "You remind me so much of myself at your age."

My father's made a living as a movie storyboard artist for fifteen years. Maybe if I'm lucky I'll get to draw for a living, too.

"See these parts here?" He points to Frank's knees and elbows in the drawing. "Getting the joints is always hard. You might want to think about using a model."

"Frank is my model," I say. "I've been watching him all afternoon."

"But Frank moves," my dad says. "A model stays in place. Using one of those small wooden mannequins could be helpful."

My ears suddenly perk up. Dad's collection of wooden mannequins sits above the cabinet in his office. When I was little, I always wanted to play with them but was told again and again they weren't toys. Was Dad now telling me that I had graduated to HIS world—the world of professional artists?

I run into his office, drag his chair across the room, and reach for several of the wooden models. One is male, another female, one is a deeper color wood and has ridges. I carry eight of them to the kitchen table and line them up. After a few minutes of examining them, I pick the one that most resembles Frank's body and start drawing. It's not that the mannequin makes the illustrating any easier, but it forces me to think about each body part individually, which definitely improves the overall drawing.

individually

My mother comes into the house carrying several bags of groceries. When she spots the mannequins lined up on the table, she lets out a low whistle. "I see Dad decided to let you into his secret stash. Lucky you." She gives me a wink, knowing how many times I've begged to play with them.

But I'm not playing with them now. I'm using them as they were meant to be used. I'm on my way to becoming a real artist.

Which ALMOST makes up for how humiliating school was today.

Matt and I Spy
on Carly

The next day is Saturday, so I don't have to worry about Umberto. Matt's brother, Jamie, gives us a ride to the skateboard shop in Santa Monica. But the skateboard shop is also the surf shop, and the first person we bump into is Carly's friend Crash. Is this what my life has come to—days just brimming with people I'd like to avoid?

I secretly watch Crash meander through the store, checking out

brimming

T-shirts and boards. He nods to Matt and me when he sees us— which is more acknowledgment than we've ever gotten from him.

acknowledgment

He's wearing his wetsuit and carrying a skateboard with graffiti on the bottom.

"He skateboards too?" Matt asks. "How come we never see him when we board?"

The most probable answer is that he's a hundred times better than we are and skateboards with older kids in places Matt and I don't even know exist. But instead of saying that out loud, I just shrug.

As Matt examines different sets of wheels, I try to act as casual as possible. "If Crash is here in his wetsuit, do you think Carly's surfing today too?"

Because the ocean's just a few

casual

blocks away, Matt and I decide to head down to the beach, which turns out to be at the bottom of a very sweet hill. We forget about finding Carly and take a dozen runs instead.

We meet two other kids who tell us this hill is where the original Dogtown boys started the whole Southern California skateboard scene. It's less than half an hour from our neighborhood, but between the sacred hill and the wide beach, it seems like we're a million miles away.

sacred

"We need to come here more often," Matt says. "Jamie could take us on his way to work."

"I can't believe Carly comes every weekend."

We slalom down the hill until we reach the bike path, then pick up our boards and walk across the sand.

Down near the lifeguard shacks, we spot a pile of towels and backpacks. I recognize Carly's purple bag immediately.

Matt and I shield our eyes from the mid-morning sun and scan the waves.

"How are we supposed to find her?" I ask. "Everybody looks the same in a wetsuit."

We search the water for several minutes until a girl on an orange board rides a wave toward shore.

"Is that her?" Matt asks. "How did she get so GOOD?"

Sure enough, the girl heading toward us is Carly, smiling and confident as she rides the wave in. She expertly jumps off her board and is about to head back out when she sees us.

expertly

"I didn't know you guys were coming to Santa Monica today." She brushes the wet hair out of her face. "The water's great. Come on in."

We explain that we don't have bathing suits, wetsuits, or surfboards. Not to mention the fact that neither Matt nor I know how to surf.

instructor

"My instructor, Heinz, has everything you need. He always has extra boards and suits in his truck."

"Your surfing instructor's name is Heinz?" I ask.

"A German surf instructor?" Matt's eyes widen. "Is Germany even near an ocean?"

Carly laughs. "His nickname's Heinz because in college he drank a bottle of ketchup on a dare. He's kind of crazy but he's a really good surf instructor." She picks up her board, untangles the leash around her ankle, and heads back to the water. "Germany IS on the water," she calls over her shoulder. "The North Sea and the Baltic Sea!"

untangles

We watch her jump back on her board. "How does she remember all that geography stuff?" I ask Matt.

"It's like she sits around memorizing a globe. Weird."

memorizing

Even as we make fun of Carly's study habits, we can't take our eyes off her as she paddles out.

"She'd kick our butts out there," I say.

"Totally," Matt agrees.

And for the first time since we've been friends, I suddenly feel as if Carly's outgrown us.

School Is Now
a Torture Zone

I spend the rest of the weekend working on my comic strip, using Dad's mannequins to help with my technique. My father thinks they've improved Frank's proportions in the drawings; I'm just happy he's entrusted me with his models.

I line up the panels on the kitchen table for my mom to see before she heads to her office. She just hired a receptionist named Judi, who takes her new puppy to work with her since he's not trained yet. I've been helping out a few times a day by walking Snickers around the block while Judi handles the phones for Mom's veterinary practice, which is right next door to our house. With Bodi, Frank, and now Snickers, our home sometimes feels like an urban menagerie.

menagerie

"These look great," my mom says.

I pray she doesn't bring up my lettering.

"I've got a great crime for Super Frank to solve," she suggests. "How about if he figures out who set off the explosion in your bedroom?"

Leave it to my mom to turn a conversation about my awesome

comic strip into a suggestion to clean my room. I tell her I'll get right on it, which really means I have no plans to get to it anytime soon.

I pack up my drawings and head to school.

Why am I worried about this new kid anyway? He's a transfer student, and I've been with most of the kids in our class since kindergarten. HE'S the one who should be worried, not me.

$$A = B$$

isosceles

maniacal

"Derek, my man," Umberto says as he wheels his chair behind his desk.

Be friendly, I think. *Don't let him get to you.*

I open my math book, probably for the first time in my life without being told to. I pretend to study the isosceles triangles until I hear maniacal laughter.

"These are hilarious," Umberto says.

When I look over, Umberto's got my comic panels spread out on his desk.

"Those were in my folder," I say. "Stop going through my stuff!"

Although I don't like the invasion of privacy, I DO like someone laughing at my comic strips. Before I know what I'm doing, I find myself fishing for a compliment.

invasion

"So you think they're funny?" I ask.

compliment

Umberto holds up the first page and points to Super Frank. "They're REALLY funny."

"Thanks."

"Is this supposed to be a monkey? It looks like a mental patient drew it."

I grab for the paper, but Umberto pulls his arm back before I can reach

guffaw

it. "Were you trying to be ironic?" he asks. "Because Super Frank doesn't look so super to me."

Stephen, who sits behind Umberto, lets out a loud guffaw. Just as I'm about to jump out of my chair, the bell rings and Ms. McCoddle tells us to take out our reading. Umberto hands me my drawings, laughing as if he's just seen a squirrel playing piano on YouTube.

As we read, I try to concentrate on all the tips the reading specialist has given me, especially visualizing the story in my mind. I picture the boy in the book painting the fence in his front yard, but in my version of the story, the main character takes the paint and dumps it on the kid sitting beside him. I've got the kid sitting next to me. Now all I need is a bucket of paint.

Matt's out sick today. I think he's faking, but in his texts he insists he really does have the flu. So I find Carly during recess and tell her about Umberto mocking my drawings.

mocking

"What is it about you that drives him so crazy?" she asks. "He's been perfectly nice to me."

"I know—people love him!" As if to prove my point, I gesture to the other side of the yard where Umberto's got two of our classmates in stitches near the picnic tables.

"Do you think they're making fun of you?" Carly asks.

"I didn't think so before but thanks for putting that in my head. I need something new to worry about. I just want this day to end."

She reminds me it's not even ten o'clock.

The rest of the day isn't much

better. (The person in front of me at lunch gets the last slice of pizza.) When I finally gather my things at the end of the day, I'm surprised to find a piece of paper ripped out of a spiral notebook on my desk. I figure Carly took pity on me and wrote a note to cheer me up. But it's not a note; it's a drawing. Of a monkey. Wearing a cape. Hurling poop at masked bad guys running down the street with bags of money. The caption printed along the bottom reads SUPER FRANK TAKES MATTERS INTO HIS OWN HANDS.

spiral

I don't have to ask who the artist is; Umberto leans across the aisle between our desks with a giant smirk.

smirk

"You inspired me," Umberto says. "I can't wait to draw some more panels."

I make a big show of loudly crumpling the drawing and shoving it under my desk. But as the class heads out for the day, I'm only focused on one thing.

crumpling

Umberto's comic is a thousand times better than mine.

The Sad Truth

I spend the rest of the afternoon lying under the jasmine with Bodi, studying Umberto's drawing. (Yes, I pretended to forget one of my books and went back to the classroom to "retrieve" it.) Super Frank's fur looks more realistic than it does in my drawing. His arms are more anatomically correct, even after I started using Dad's mannequins. It

anatomically

HEAD
HEART
BABY TOE

kills me to admit, but the POOP in his comic looks better than mine too. The only thing that's better in my illustration is that I used a marker; Umberto's is done in regular pencil. That one fact hardly decreases my disappointment. Luckily my failure as an artist doesn't affect the way Bodi feels about me; he scrunches in beside me the way he's done since I was little. My cartooning skills don't factor into our relationship, never have. And today that means everything.

Part of me feels I should be happy for Umberto. He obviously has some excellent skills; maybe he'll have a career as an illustrator or a cartoonist. We actually have something in common and would probably be good friends—if he wasn't such a bunionhead. But everything Umberto's done since coming to our school makes me think friendship is the last thing on his mind. And if he thinks he's stealing my idea for *Super Frank*, any kind of amiable relationship is out of the question.

amiable

It turns out Matt really IS sick. When I stop over his house to show him the crumpled drawing, his mom tells me he's asleep and she doesn't want to disturb him. So I take Snickers and Bodi for several walks around the neighborhood before putting together my plan. If Umberto wants a drawing war, he's going to get one.

Like a mercenary soldier, I gather my ammunition: markers, colored pencils, erasers, ruler, drawing pads,

mercenary

ink, and pens. I may have less natural talent than Umberto but I'm not going down without a fight.

I work for the rest of the afternoon just drawing Frank's legs. When my mother calls me for dinner, I wolf down the meatloaf and head back to my room to focus on Frank's face. I keep sneaking downstairs to scrutinize Frank's body parts, taking photos to study upstairs.

scrutinize

At bedtime, my father peeks into my room. "You look like me when I'm on deadline. What are you working on?"

I tell him I want to take my drawing to the next level. "How can I run a cartoon club when I'm not even that good?"

"A club is so people can share their love of something. It doesn't mean your drawings have to be perfect."

When I tell him I just want to get better, he says it's always good to try to improve your skills. "Want some help?"

First I tell him no, then change my mind and ask him if Frank's eyes look realistic enough. He grabs a fresh piece of paper and shows me several ways I can shade the pupils to make Frank's eyes come alive. Umberto may have more raw talent, but I have a mentor.

mentor

"It doesn't just take technical skill to be a cartoonist," my dad says. "A big part of the job is finding humor in everyday situations, too."

He takes out a *Calvin and Hobbes* from my bookcase, as well as a few *Garfields*. He points out several strips and explains how the artists took routine things like homework and lasagna and made them important parts of the characters' worlds. We sit on my bed for almost an hour going through the books before it hits me: *I'm studying comics! This is the best job in the world!*

By the time I go to bed, the last thing on my mind is some kid who's trying to make me miserable. Instead, I'm confident I'll be able to keep improving to make *Super Frank* the best comic strip it can be.

Bodi circles the floor next to my bed and settles in for the night. Reading comics with my dad AND sleeping next to my dog? Umberto's got nothing on me today.

The Real Frank Goes on an Adventure

The next day is a professional day where the teachers have meetings and kids thankfully don't have to go to school. My mom says our teachers do stuff like examine the curriculum and talk about homework and tests, but I think they secretly run through the halls laughing and screaming because they never get to let loose while the school is full of kids. I bet

curriculum

they have a giant food fight in the cafeteria, then use the corridor like a Slip 'N Slide to glide on gravy from one end of the school to the other. My mother listens to this scenario patiently until I get to the part where Principal Demetri lights the make-shift luge on fire with a giant blowtorch he keeps underneath his desk. I can tell she's no longer listening because her eyes are closed, just waiting for me to finish.

blowtorch

"I can keep going if you want me to," I say.

Mom puts up her hand to stop me. "How about if you do your homework—"

"It's a vacation day!"

"Technically, it's NOT a vacation day. Your teachers have meetings. You spent so much time drawing yesterday that you didn't study for your math test."

I don't understand how my mom can run a successful veterinary business, manage seven employees, take care of hundreds of dogs, cats, and birds, as well as the occasional ferret, AND monitor every minute detail of my six classes. Not to mention taking care of the house, the food, and all that other stuff I don't want to think about. It makes me wonder if she's secretly got several Mom Clones stashed in the garage that she's programmed to carry out various jobs throughout the day.

programmed

"How about if you study for half an hour," she suggests. "Then you can have the rest of the day to yourself."

She says this like it's good news,

eternity

limitless

as if half an hour of math doesn't define the word *eternity*.

"How's it going with illustrating your vocabulary words?" she asks.

"I didn't realize I had the day off so I could be interrogated," I answer.

At this point, my mother gives up, as I hoped she would. (The older she gets, the easier it is to wear her down. Lucky for me, my energy for such tasks is limitless.)

As my mother takes Frank out of the cage and hands him to me, she doesn't have to tell me he needs to be changed; anyone with a sense of smell would come to the same conclusion. I go next door to her office to change him on one of the large tables. On the way back, I grab a dog biscuit from the receptionist's desk to give to Bodi.

Matt's still sick, so I skateboard by myself around the neighborhood, then head to UCLA. There's some kind of worker protest at the quad, which I hang around to watch until the whole thing makes me hungry and I head back home.

When I take Frank out of his cage later, he immediately runs up my arm and sits on my shoulder. Even though we're a foster family and we're technically not supposed to train him, I've taught Frank several basic skills he can use when he graduates to being a companion for someone with physical challenges. I haven't taught him anything difficult, like opening water bottles or dialing a phone, but I have taught him how to open a DVD case and take out the disc. It took me a week of

challenges

opening and closing DVD cases, but Frank eventually accomplished the task. Just to keep him in practice, I find an action movie in the den and hand it to Frank as I make myself a peanut butter and banana sandwich. He opens the case in no time flat and takes out the DVD.

I use the last of the peanut butter, scraping my knife along the edge of the jar to get the bits along the side. I'm not two bites into my sandwich when I turn around to find Frank with his head inside the jar.

"Frank! What are you doing? There's no peanut butter in there!"

But Frank can't hear me; his head is wedged inside the jar and he can't get it off. He flails around the kitchen, looking like one of those

wedged

astronaut monkeys the Russians shot into space in the 1950s.

I try to calm Frank down, but he's running around the kitchen, unable to see. The commotion upsets Bodi, who begins to bark. It's just a matter of time before someone from my mother's office comes over to check on the noise. I hurry to catch Frank before they do.

commotion

I use my best sing-song voice to get Frank's attention but it doesn't work. I try to grab him, but now he's up on the counter, shrieking.

"What's going on here?"

I turn and find my father standing in the doorway. He tells the person on the other end of his cell that he'll call him back.

Together the two of us slowly and calmly walk toward Frank. My father gets to the left of him, I get to the right and gently grab him as he tries to jump onto the cabinet. I hold Frank steady while my father carefully removes the jar from his head.

Frank's fur is now covered in a helmet of peanut butter.

"Let me guess," my father says. "You were playing space man? Or is this an undersea adventure?"

I make a mental note about a potential adventure game to be played at a later date and tell Dad the whole thing was 100 percent accident. I can tell he's weighing my answer, trying to decide whether or not to believe me. While he does, he fills up the sink with sudsy water.

"You have to give Frank a bath," Dad says.

I tell him no problem, not just

because Frank is filthy but because giving a monkey a bath is a chore I actually like. Bodi's already licked a lot of the peanut butter off Frank's fur. I pick up Frank from the floor, remove his diaper, and place him cautiously in the sink.

I'm eternally grateful that my father doesn't lecture me on the danger of cylindrical objects and instead just stands next to me at the sink, helping me spray down our monkey.

cylindrical

"I'm going to miss him when it's time for the capuchin organization to take him back," my dad says. "He's almost part of the family now."

"But we've got him for at least a few more months, don't we?"

"I guess it depends on how many people they have on their waiting list."

quivers

harassment

My body suddenly quivers as if I've just been struck by a bolt of lightning. As I wrap Frank in a towel, I realize my initial idea to tell Umberto about Frank was correct. I've let myself be derailed by Umberto's harassment; I've got to get back on track. A monkey helper is the perfect olive branch to offer Umberto, a way to turn him from bully to friend in two seconds flat.

I set to work on my new plan of training Frank to be Umberto's companion.

The Perfect Monkey Friend

I find all the brochures and DVDs from the monkey organization in a box in Dad's office. I tell him I want to study up on what Frank will learn after he leaves us, but what I really want to do is scour the information to see if Umberto would be a good applicant to receive a monkey helper.

Even though it's not a school day, I don't complain about all the reading and make myself comfortable on the floor of the den, Bodi by my side. It takes a while to get through the material but I learn several things. The training Frank will be attending is called monkey college and will last about three years. He'll learn how to fetch various objects around the house, adjust someone's glasses, turn the pages of a book, scratch someone's itch—awesome!— even reposition someone's arms and feet. I've been so proud of Frank for being able to open and close a DVD case that I didn't realize how many other tasks he'll have to master.

reposition

After applicants fill out the twelve-page (!!!) form, it might take a year before finding out if they are eligible for a monkey helper. But if they do get one, their relationship can last for years. Like my friend Michael who's been with Pedro for almost a decade, Umberto might benefit from having more help around the house.

I take out my pad and make a list of all the steps Umberto will have to take to make this happen. Even if it does seem insurmountable, within a year Umberto could be hanging out with a super-cool monkey friend. I'd no longer be the cartoonist in the next desk that he hates but the kid who got him a MONKEY. I text Matt that he has nothing more to worry about, that I've taken care of what he calls THE UMBERTO SITUATION by coming up with a new and improved idea.

On a vacation day!

insurmountable

Not the Reaction
I Planned On

Matt's back in school, but class hasn't even started yet and he already has a slimy stripe on the sleeve of his shirt from wiping his nose on it.

"I look worse than I am," he says. "I could've come over yesterday but I wanted to see if I could beat my own record."

Since Matt got a Wii for his birthday a few months ago, he's played more golf and tennis than a country club kid. Matt says the games are building good hand-eye coordination, but I'm not so sure he'd rack up as many points with a real golf club or tennis racket.

coordination

"I can't believe your plan is to offer up Frank to your mortal enemy," Matt says.

I explain that as much as Umberto's been a giant pain in the butt, he's not my nemesis. "As far as giving up Frank, we have only a few months more with him before he has to go to monkey college anyway."

nemesis

"That's probably where you'll end up going to school too."

I ignore Matt's lame joke. "At least if Frank's with Umberto, I'd get to visit him."

"In your demented mind, Frank

congested

suddenly makes Umberto like you and you're hanging out at his house with Frank. Is that it?"

I wonder if Matt is trying to be difficult or if he's so congested, his brain has finally shut down. "I'm just saying if Frank ends up with some guy in Montana, I'll probably never see him again."

"I knew there had to be an ulterior motive," Matt coughs. "You're not the Mother Teresa type."

I tell him Mother Teresa worked mostly with lepers, which is what he's going to be if he keeps coughing his lungs out.

When I get to my desk, I'm surprised to find several panels with neat illustrations waiting for me. My gasp is audible when I read the title of the strip: *Super Hank.*

audible

I don't have to ask who the artist is—the illustration style is familiar. I can feel my blood begin to boil.

Umberto's strip also stars a monkey but instead of a cape like Super Frank, he's wearing a trench coat and a hat. The dialogue is neatly printed and snappy, like the old black-and-white gangster movies my uncle Bob likes to watch.

gangster

"What do you think?" Umberto asks.

I tell him it's a complete rip-off of my comic strip.

Umberto wheels himself over to my desk. "What are you talking about? Hank is short for Henry. That's a totally different name than Frank."

By now, Matt and Carly have joined us. Carly holds up the pages and examines them. "It's too bad you couldn't come up with your own idea, Umberto," she says. "I'm sure there are lots of other characters you could've created besides a superhero monkey."

"He's not a superhero," Umberto says. "He's a detective. Completely different."

I stare at the pages while a million thoughts ricochet in my head. Why did Umberto choose ME to pick on? Why do his drawings look so good? WHY WAS I GOING TO HELP HIM ADOPT MY MONKEY?

My initial reaction is to rip Umberto's precious drawings to shreds, but as an illustrator, I know how hard he probably worked on them and can't bring myself to do it. Instead, I dangle the pages over

Umberto's head. "You want them? Come and get them."

From his wheelchair, Umberto tries to reach them but can't.

"Um, maybe you should just give them back," Carly suggests.

But I'm having too much fun watching Umberto struggle.

"Derek Fallon!" Ms. McCoddle shouts. "What on earth is going on?"

Before I can answer, she snatches the pages from my hands and gives them to Umberto, who's still trying to reach them. The expression on his face is that of a hungry street urchin. Forget comics; this kid should join the drama club.

urchin

I try to explain but Ms. McCoddle cuts me off. "I want to see you after class," she says.

"Both of us?" Umberto asks in a

angelic

voice that can only be called angelic.

Ms. McCoddle points straight at me. "Just Derek."

Matt pretends to hang himself with an invisible rope, and Carly just shakes her head.

"I know Umberto started it," she whispers. "But it looked really bad, like you were taunting a kid in a wheelchair."

Carly doesn't need to remind me—I can only imagine how the whole scene appeared. I remember Michael telling me about two guys at a Dodgers game who made fun of him, eventually grabbing his pack and playing catch with it. He couldn't stop them, couldn't do anything to retaliate from his wheelchair. The fact that for just a moment I looked like those guys makes me feel

retaliate

terrible—not to mention that I'm also counting down the minutes till Ms. McCoddle lowers the boom.

Ms. McCoddle doesn't even look at me when she hands out the math test.

This wasn't how I thought today would go when I got up this morning.

Ms. McCoddle
Plays Hardball

I have a detailed explanation ready
to give Ms. McCoddle but she cuts
me off at the knees.

"Derek, I don't know what's
gotten into you lately."

hothead

I rein in my anger and try not to
look like a hothead.

"This only started happening
when Umberto transferred into our
class," I say. "He's been egging me
on, looking for trouble."

"Really? Because from what I saw today, YOU were the one starting the conflict."

I look down at my sneakers, feeling suddenly awkward. "You've known me since kindergarten—I'm not someone who looks for trouble."

awkward

Ms. McCoddle softens a bit. "Umberto had good grades at his last school with no discipline problems. Plus, he seems like a nice kid. So I suggest you two come to some sort of understanding before things get out of hand."

As she talks, she stands on a chair and pins up posters of penguins and glaciers, getting ready for the section we're starting on Antarctica. I try to get on her good side by handing her thumbtacks.

"Kids with various disabilities sometimes have it tougher than

irritated

other kids," Ms. McCoddle says. "You should know that."

I'm irritated she's bringing up my poor reading skills as a way to force a connection between Umberto and me. I hold the thumbtack too far for her to reach and watch her wobble on the chair.

"Everyone has obstacles to overcome," she continues. "You and Umberto might have a lot in common after all."

"Why aren't you giving HIM this lecture?" I ask as I finally give her the thumbtack. "He's the one going out of his way to stir up trouble."

She carefully climbs off the chair, weighing her words. "I'm telling you because I know you. I'm asking you, as a favor, to smooth things out."

Ms. McCoddle smiles at me now

with such warmth that she could almost melt the ice in the photos behind her.

comply

I decide to comply with her wishes and point to the collage. "How come you didn't put up any polar bears?"

"Polar bears live in the Arctic, at the North Pole. The only time they're near penguins is at the zoo."

Thankfully, she doesn't give me grief about not doing the reading or knowing my geography. I head to my locker, determined to set things right with Umberto even if he's the one who's been instigating all the trouble. I just hope we're not like penguins and polar bears—thousands of miles away from each other with nothing to connect us but ice.

instigating

Comedy Club

Between my talk with Ms. McCoddle and cartoon club starting this week, I push my troubles with Umberto to the back of my mind. Five kids have signed up, but thankfully not Umberto. Since Matt's club is on Tuesday and mine's on Thursday, I help him prepare for his first. He finds several clips in his giant DVD collection, then puts them into different categories: action comedies, buddy comedies, horror comedies, gross-out comedies, fish-out-of-water comedies. All the work he's put into his club makes me wonder if I'm prepared enough for mine.

categories

"Eight kids have signed up. Do you think that's enough?" Matt asks.

I tell him my club has even less. "Besides, once word gets out how funny your club is, you'll have more kids wanting to join."

"Do you think Mr. Owens will be okay?" Matt asks. "He's not the first teacher you think of when you think *funny*."

I stop in my tracks. "You're actually WORRIED about this? You're not supposed to get stressed out about comedy."

"I just want everything to be good," Matt says. "You know how Mr. Owens likes to comment on everything all the time."

I remind Matt that every after-school club needs a teacher to monitor it, and Mr. Owens was the only one who agreed to help. "Everything's going to be fine. You can't go wrong with comedy."

I feel as if I've actually acted like a good best friend because Matt calms down as we head to the classroom he's reserved.

The usual suspects are there—Pete, Bobby, Runt, and Sam—as well as two girls I hadn't met before, Heather and Wendy.

Mr. Owens rubs his hands together like he's standing in front of a campfire. "Are you ready to get

monitor

this show on the road? And when I say *road* I mean ROAD MOVIE!" He holds up the DVD to a movie Matt and I hate, and I suddenly realize Matt was right to worry about Mr. Owens being overly involved.

"Actually, Mr. Owens, we're not doing that movie today," Matt says.

assertive

I'm proud Matt's being assertive instead of just going along with Mr. Owens because he's a teacher.

Mr. Owens waves the DVD box in the air. "No problem. This is your show. I'll be back at my desk grading papers. Let me know if you need someone to bail you out."

Matt leans against a desk in the front row and addresses the kids who've come today. "Okay, let's start with buddy movies."

He takes a marker and makes a

suppress

heckle

list of buddy comedies on the Smart Board behind him. It's funny to see Matt acting so teacher-y. I have to suppress my initial reaction to heckle him and sit quietly instead, especially since our positions will be reversed for my class in a few days.

"You left out a few classics," Mr. Owens pipes up from the back of the room.

I watch as Matt decides whether to include Mr. Owens in the conversation or keep going. To my surprise, he plows straight ahead, ignoring him. "Let's talk about the two main characters in a buddy movie and how they're usually opposites."

"Not always," Mr. Owens says. "But it makes for better conflict if they are."

Matt leans his head against the Smart Board. I know he wants to tell Mr. Owens to shut up but, of course, he can't. I try to help by asking about one of the movies on the list.

"Do you have a clip from that one?" I ask, knowing full well he does.

"Good idea. Let's go to a clip." Matt plays a few scenes from the buddy movie on his laptop, which he's connected to the projector. Soon everyone's laughing and back on track.

Mr. Owens focuses on his work for the rest of the hour and it's obvious when everyone gets up to leave they enjoyed Matt's club.

"Next week, holiday comedies." As Matt gathers up his notes, I can tell

brainstorming

he's happy with his accomplishment, already brainstorming ideas for future meetings.

We rush out of the room before Mr. Owens finishes with his papers so we don't have to listen to his suggestions.

"He's just supposed to be in the room," Matt says as we head to our lockers. "He's not supposed to *contribute*."

Ms. Ramirez, the art teacher, is monitoring my club on Thursday; Ms. McCoddle offered to do it but the principal decided to appoint her as head of the English Committee, basically canceling all her free time. I pray Ms. Ramirez is less intrusive than Mr. Owens. But what makes me come to a grinding halt isn't the thought of Ms. Ramirez ruining my

intrusive

club but what I see at the end of the hallway. Matt also stops, both of us frozen in front of the science lab.

"Is that . . . Carly?" Matt whispers.

I nod, too surprised to form words.

"Kissing Crash?!"

We silently back up the hall before Carly sees us.

Carly Has a Boyfriend?!

inconceivable

"It's inconceivable!" I say when we get outside.

"You mean it's inconceivable that Carly has a boyfriend and it isn't YOU?" Matt adds.

"What are you talking about? I didn't say that."

Matt shoves his index cards into his backpack. "No, I'M saying that. You've had a crush on her from Day One."

"Are you kidding?" I yell. "We HATED her in the beginning!"

"I mean after we became friends with her, whatever day that was." He zips up his pack. "If you don't like her, then why do you care?"

"Don't make this about me. You're as shocked as I am she's making out with Crash."

Matt smirks, as if getting me upset is part of his master plan. "I'm surprised she's with Crash, but I'm not half as upset as you are."

"I AM NOT UPSET!"

This statement is so ludicrous I have no choice but to join Matt in his laughter.

"I'm just shocked. I mean, Crash is so—"

"—Much cooler than we are?" Matt interrupts.

I don't admit to Matt that the

reason I'm having a hard time with Carly going out with Crash isn't because the guy's too cool but because he's actually *nice.*

I don't often work in my mother's office but one day last year I was helping her organize some samples when Crash came in with his father and their cat that wouldn't stop scratching. As I watched from the hall, an older woman came out of one of the exam rooms, crying because her dog had just been put to sleep. My mother had her arm around the woman as she headed toward the exit. The woman told my mom she was fine but when she started crying all over again, it was Crash who jumped up from his seat to grab the woman's arm and help her to the door. I was nearby but,

I'm ashamed to admit, frozen by the woman's grief. It's easy for Matt and me to make fun of Crash but I know there's more to him than just his surfer vocabulary and skateboarding skills.

ashamed

"Hey, guys! What are you still doing here?"

Matt and I freeze at the sound of Carly's voice. Thankfully she's by herself.

Matt tells her today was the debut of his comedy club. While he discusses the class, I check Carly out with new eyes. She is smart and her newfound confidence from surfing has made her more attractive too. Her hair is lighter from all the time she's spending outside.

Neither Matt nor I have ever gone

milestone

out with anyone; I guess I never thought Carly would beat us to that milestone. I try not to think of her differently as she talks to Matt now, but I have to admit, I do.

"You want to get some frozen yogurt?" she asks.

Matt gives me a look, asking me what I think. I say sure and we head toward Wilshire. We talk about the shocking piles of homework Ms. Decker's been handing out and how Swifty had to get stitches on his forehead after tripping in a puddle of his own sweat in gym class. As I watch Carly do her impersonation of Swifty, all I can think of is Crash— and how lucky he is to have Carly as a girlfriend.

Lots of Preparation

The next few days I'm so focused on preparing for cartoon club that I fail a math test and forget to walk Snickers, who ends up peeing all over the rug in Mom's office. Neither of these events bothers me much but I do feel bad about missing time with Bodi. He's been more lethargic than usual, so I promise myself to spend some time with him after Thursday's meeting.

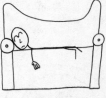

lethargic

As I told Ms. McCoddle, Ms. Ramirez, and anyone else who'd listen, I hardly consider myself an illustration expert; I just want to talk about drawing cartoons. Two of the kids who signed up—Terry and Tommy, identical twins who I've never been in class with—do these hilarious drawings of cats with bloodshot eyes and razor-like claws that I've seen plastered around school. My guess is that they were influenced by *Ren and Stimpy*, and I can't wait to talk to them about it.

influenced

I put together an outline for the six weeks the club will run and include topics like developing characters and layout. For an instant, I consider having my father come in as a guest lecturer, but since he's my dad and I'm trying to project an aura of independence, I decide against it.

aura

In the section on materials, I write down all the different options most comic book artists use: markers, pen and ink, pencils, erasers, and quality paper. I break down the different stages of comic book art into outlining, inking, coloring, and lettering. I've always done all stages myself as I'm sure most of the other kids have, although I'd KILL to have someone else do my lettering. Maybe some of the other kids will have tips they can share on how to get the lettering in my strips to look professional instead of like it was done by a psychotic toddler.

psychotic

When I'm finished, I check the latest sign-up sheet. Even though neither Matt nor Carly is interested in cartooning, both of them have registered for the class to be supportive. I'm especially happy that

Carly is coming; I was worried she'd try to weasel out of it to spend more time with Crash. But one thing about Carly, she's a solid friend.

exhaustively

Of course the real reason I'm exhaustively checking the list is to make sure Umberto didn't sign up at the last minute. I close all the files for the club on my computer and breathe a sigh of relief.

The rest of the night I spend happily sandwiched between Bodi and Frank on the couch. My mother hates it when I let them up on the furniture, but she's doing paperwork in her office and Dad doesn't mind as much as she does. As we watch the sitcom family on TV, Dad reminds me of what we talked about recently—how normal, routine things can become the topic of a

comic strip. But my brain is fried.
The last thing on my mind is milking
this moment for material. Instead, I
lean my head against the cushion
and enjoy the moment for what it is:
perfect.

Today's the Day

After class I hurry to Ms. Ramirez's art room on the other side of the school.

"I'm not going to say a peep. This is your show," Ms. Ramirez assures me. She's wearing a scarf around her neck that's wrapped so many times I wonder if I'm going to have to save her from asphyxiation.

"Feel free to use any of the materials in the room," Ms. Ramirez

asphyxiation

continues. "Make yourself at home."

She's being so accommodating and friendly, I feel bad for worrying about her so much.

accommodating

Matt comes in and tosses his stuff on the first desk. "You're not going to give homework, are you? Cuz the last thing I need is to start drawing stick figures on everything the way you do."

I make sure Ms. Ramirez isn't looking, then hurl an eraser at Matt. He brushes the chalk off his jeans with a laugh. The two of us stop fooling around when we see Carly hovering outside the class-room door . . . with Crash.

Matt leans over and whispers to me. "Where does he think she's going—Hawaii? The club's only an hour. Can't they live without each other for that long?"

I'm so busy watching Carly's body language that I barely listen to Matt. She's twirling her hair, throwing her head back, and laughing at something that doesn't sound remotely funny. What is happening to her? Just as I'm about to gag at Carly turning into some airhead girlfriend, Matt smacks me with the eraser.

"Dude, wake up! You've got a club to run."

He's right. I take my place in the front of the room and try not to fixate on Carly when she finally joins us.

I open my pad and check my notes. "I want to welcome everyone to the first meeting of the cartoon drawing club. We're going to have a lot of fun."

I look around the room at Matt, Carly, Terry, Tommy, and Susan, who

fixate

I don't know but already looks bored. "I thought we could start by checking out what we'll be talking about for the next six weeks." I take a stack of pages from my pack and pass them out.

"Handouts!" Matt jokes. "You went all out."

Carly laughs and for a moment it's as if it's just the three of us, goofing around in BC time—Before Crash.

"Today's topic is creating original characters," I continue.

"Speaking of original characters, any room for me?"

I don't need to look to see whose voice that is. Umberto wheels himself into the room with a flourish. "I didn't sign up. I hope you don't mind walk-ins."

Everyone in the room stops what

flourish

they're doing to process Umberto's joke. Finally Susan bursts out laughing, then the other kids do too. Matt and Carly check to see how I'll react but I just laugh along with the others. What I really feel inside isn't delight but dread. *Has Umberto made it his life's work to torture me?* If so, he's doing a bang-up job.

I muster all my strength to bring the club back on track and hand Umberto a copy of the class outline. "We're talking about creating characters. I thought Terry and Tommy could talk about the cat comic strips they do."

"Can't wait," Umberto says. "After that, I want to talk about my monkey strip."

"Cool," Terry says. "I love monkeys."

muster

Umberto reaches into his pack and pulls out a stack of papers. *This is not happening.*

"These are awesome," Tommy says. "Using a monkey is a great idea."

I stare at my pack on the desk. My own work will now look like a replica of Umberto's. The kid hasn't been in the room for a minute and he's already succeeded in taking the wind out of my sails.

replica

Even though she's been focused on Crash 24/7, Carly immediately comes to my rescue. "Can we see the cats?" she asks the twins. "They sound really great."

Tommy and Terry each take out stacks of wrinkled pages from their packs. I try to grab the reins of the class back by asking how they

unsettled

originally came up with the idea. When I spy Umberto out of the corner of my eye, he's not as unsettled as I'd hoped, but instead listens to Terry with full attention.

Tommy talks about how the cat character has evolved since they first started drawing him but Terry interrupts him. "What about you, Derek? Show us some of your illustrations."

I reluctantly spread my *Super Frank* panels across the desk.

"These are great!" Matt says, as if it's the first time he's seen them. "Super Frank looks like a real monkey."

Susan takes one of my drawings and compares it to Umberto's. "Your monkey has much better fur," she tells him. "The face is more realistic, too."

"Yeah, and the lettering's really professional," Tommy adds.

"I worked hard on them," says Umberto proudly.

Starting a cartooning club suddenly seems like the idea of an imbecile—namely, me.

"I think Derek's are more original," Carly says. "Having a baby seal as a bad guy is totally unexpected."

unexpected

Just about as unexpected as a classmate in a wheelchair trying to ruin your life, I think. But the other kids want to hear more about Umberto's process. I admit defeat and give up trying to manage the club, at least for this session. Umberto has conquered me fair and square. I sit down next to Matt, who shrugs. He's right—Umberto's won this round; it's up to me to win the next one.

Water on the Brain

After the fiasco with the cartoon club, all I want to do is hole up in a cave, but Carly won't have it. She convinces Matt the best medicine is for me to go surfing. She arranges for Heinz to give us lessons at an introductory rate. Matt's wanted to try surfing for a long time and immediately says yes for the two of us.

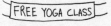

introductory

Matt's brother, Jamie, drops us

off in Santa Monica, where Carly, Crash, and some other kids are already getting ready to go out. It doesn't take a genius to guess which one is Heinz. The guy's so tan and his hair so bleached from the sun, he looks like he hasn't spent a minute of his life indoors. He calls Matt and me over to his truck and throws us each a wetsuit.

"You guys are totally getting up today," Heinz says. "I guarantee it."

Matt and I explain that we're skateboarders who've never been surfing before.

"Skateboarding will really help with your balance," Heinz says. "But it's all about the pop-up." He explains that the most important thing is going from a paddle position to a standing position—fast. He chooses two surfboards from several in his van and tells us to meet him by the water.

As Matt and I walk down the beach, I look around to locate Carly, but she and Crash have already paddled out.

"You think we'll really catch a ride today?" Matt asks. "That would be awesome."

I try not to get my hopes up; if surfing turns out to be anything like the cartoon club, I'll end up tangled up in my leash, spit up on the shore with a face full of sand.

When my parents asked me last night how the club went, I told them it was amazing, that the other kids got a lot out of it too. I may have gone a bit over the top, animatedly describing the club's camaraderie.

camaraderie

undermined

authority

Dad seemed proud that the information he'd shared had been useful; I didn't want to spoil his good feelings by admitting Umberto had undermined my comics as well as my authority.

The truth is I couldn't just blame Umberto; I LET my authority as the club's leader be undermined. I could've guided the club back on track after Umberto tried to take over but I didn't, choosing the easier path of surrender. And that was the part that hurt more than Umberto staking claim to my comic book ideas.

Thankfully, I can't spend the morning dwelling on past mistakes because Heinz has us in the sand practicing pop-ups. Going from lying down to standing as fast as you can isn't a skateboard skill. But after twenty minutes of practicing, Matt and I seem to get the hang of it. When I look out on the horizon to find Carly in the water, she and Crash are sitting on their boards talking, framed by the morning sun.

"Today's a good day to learn," Heinz says. "Not a lot of wind and nice, easy waves." He motions for us to grab our boards and follow him out.

When Carly sees us, she yells some much needed encouragement.

"I knew those two would hit it off." Heinz gestures to Carly and Crash. "They're like two peas in a pod."

Matt shoots me a "what is he talking about?" look. I could tell him

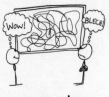

perspective

I've got a different perspective on Crash but I don't, letting Matt continue our game of Trash Crash. "Crash and Carly made for each other—as if!" he says.

"Yeah, what do we know? We're only her best friends," I add.

The water's cold at first. Heinz walks alongside us as Matt and I paddle out. With new sets of waves coming at faster intervals, getting outside-the-break is more difficult than it looks. It's hard to imagine Carly's gotten so good so fast; she breezes by us effortlessly.

"Okay," Heinz says. He's standing chest-deep in the water between us. "It takes a while to learn how to read the waves. So for now you'll have to trust me on which waves are the best ones for you to catch."

I'm not sure how advisable it is to put your faith in a guy who got his nickname chugging a bottle of ketchup, but that's what Matt and I do.

chugging

"Not this one," Heinz says when Matt impatiently starts to go. He brings Matt's board parallel to mine. "Sometimes the most important skill to have out here is patience."

After a few minutes, Heinz turns to me. "This next one—go!" And before I can ask a single question, he pushes my board, with me on it, toward the shore.

I pop up immediately, completing phase one of today's lesson. All I have to do now is stay on the board, which I do for approximately half a second before I fall off and get sucked under the water.

approximately

clobbered

addicted

I don't worry about losing the board—it's connected to my ankle by a leash—just getting clobbered by it. After being tossed around by the ocean for several seconds, I break through the surface and take a deep breath of fresh air.

Even though I've just been flung around by the waves and didn't ride more than a few inches, it's obvious how people can get addicted to this sport. Granted, I failed miserably in my first attempt BUT I LOVED IT.

I turn around when I hear Heinz yelling at Matt to go. Matt pops up like a champ—a little slower than I did—but unlike me, he stays up. My best friend rides his very first wave all the way into shore. I'd be lying if I didn't admit to feeling a tiny bit envious.

When he emerges from the water, I'm right there waiting for him.

"You were amazing!" I shout. "You rode it all the way in!"

Matt lets out a yell and tugs the leash to bring his board closer. "Let's go again!"

Heinz calls us back out. Even though he's probably fifty yards away and we have to fight the wind and waves to get to him, neither Matt nor I complain as we paddle back out. It takes me four more attempts before I finally ride a wave all the way to shore.

attempts

"You guys were great!" Carly tells us afterward. Her hair falls around her face in little blond spirals.

"Not bad for your first time," Crash says.

Matt and I exchange glances. The fact that Crash is even talking to us—never mind giving us a compliment—is almost more than either of us could hope for.

"I'm going to stay," Crash tells Carly. "Why don't you go with your friends?"

"I can stay too." Carly looks at him expectantly.

expectantly

Both Matt and I dig around in our packs for money to pay Heinz, trying to ignore the private conversation going on around us.

"Freddy just texted me," Crash continues. "I'm going to meet him at the shop later." He gives Carly a quick kiss, then heads down to the water.

I can tell by the way her face falls that Carly doesn't want Crash to leave. She looks out over the parking lot, unsure of what to do.

"Hey, let's get some of those famous chicken wings you keep talking about," I tell her.

She nods and follows us as we bring our boards to Heinz's truck. But the usual chatty Carly doesn't say a word.

"You should definitely come with us," Matt adds. "In case Derek didn't bring enough money."

A part of Carly looks like she wants to laugh, but most of her still looks sad. "I just thought Crash and I would spend the day together, that's all."

"Sorry we're such a lame second prize," I respond.

She elbows me in the side. "I didn't say THAT." She takes off, sprinting up the hill, daring us to catch up with her.

It's hardly a contest, but Matt and I hold ourselves back so Carly can win.

An Empty Club

At the next cartoon club, I'm appalled that the only other member there besides me is Matt. I knew Carly had an eye doctor appointment and wouldn't be here. But where is everyone else?

appalled

"Was the first class that bad?" I ask Matt. "Is that why no one's here?"

Ms. Ramirez answers for him.

"Attendance usually drops off after the first session. Happens in all the clubs. Kids get bored so easily nowadays."

"Bored with CARTOONS?" The concept hardly seems possible.

begrudgingly

attentively

I begrudgingly go to the class outline, putting a smile on my face as I tell Matt we're going to talk about creating characters. Like any good best friend, he listens attentively, even when I lose my place twice.

Half an hour into the meeting, Tommy and Terry show up.

"Sorry," Tommy says. "There was a band meeting we couldn't get out of."

As they grab their seats, I feel a bit relieved. Why do I always think everything's about me? The other kids who aren't here probably have good excuses too. With new vitality, I go back to today's topic, using examples from my own notebooks to share. My drawings cover the desk like a cartoon tablecloth. Everything's going well . . . until Umberto wheels himself in.

vitality

"I didn't know today was show-and-tell," he says. "Or I would've brought copies for everyone." He reaches for the pack slung on the back of his chair. "Oh wait. I did!"

He takes a stack of homemade comic books out of his bag and passes them around. In two seconds flat, Umberto has completely deflected the group's attention from my work to his. I flip through his handout with the lame, unoriginal Super Hank until I spot his copycat

deflected

hero capturing two terrorists who just happen to be...baby seals.

I can barely control my anger. "Are you kidding me? This is a total rip-off!"

Umberto shoots me a canary-eating grin. "Why? Is my strip similar to yours?"

"You know it is! Either that or two people who just happen to sit next to each other in class both come up with bad guys who are baby seals."

Umberto looks at me with an expression of mock innocence. "My bad guys are sea lions, which are totally different from baby seals. Sea lions have ears. They're social and spend a lot of time out of the water—"

"I don't care about sea lions!" I find myself shouting. "First you copied my monkey, then you copied my seal! You wouldn't know an original idea if it bit you in the butt!"

"That would never happen," Umberto laughs. "Considering my butt is always stuck in this chair."

Yet again Umberto's managed to turn an innocent comment into a crack about his disability. I have to hand it to him—he outsmarts me every time.

defuse

Matt tries to defuse the situation by asking Tommy to tell me about the new ink he found. As Tommy discusses how much better his lettering's been since he discovered the new ink, my mind projects several years into the future to Umberto and me battling it out in caps and gowns at high school graduation with him trying to run me over with his wheelchair as I accept my diploma.

quarrel

I'm determined not to let the other kids suffer because of my quarrel with Umberto, so I steer the conversation back to the class outline.

The rest of the class goes by quickly and I'm surprised when Ms. Ramirez announces it's four o'clock.

Umberto looks over as I pack up my drawings. "These really are good," he says. "Too bad I thought of mine first."

For once I decide to listen to Carly's advice and not take the bait.

"Ready, Matt?" I ask.

Umberto blocks my path. "Hey, George. I'm talking to you."

I continue to ignore him, which seems to make him even madder. I look up to see if Ms. Ramirez is still here but she's in the hall talking to Mrs. Taylor.

"Hey, Derek," Matt says. "Our ride is here."

I hurry past Umberto to Matt in the doorway. I know he's lying— we're walking home today, not getting a ride—but I appreciate Matt trying to extract me from the situation.

extract

"You can run, but you can't hide," Umberto calls after me. "Unlike me, who can't run at all."

Outside, I thank Matt for bailing me out.

"You need a new strategy," Matt says. "Umberto's only getting worse."

I nod, knowing it's true.

"Let's go to my house," he says. "I've got a package of hot dogs with your name on it."

Anyone else would think Matt is

suggesting an early dinner, but I know better. When we get to his house, he takes the hot dogs out of the fridge and gets a ball of thick twine from the garage. We cut the string into four-inch lengths, then get a nail to poke holes into the top of each hot dog. Using the glue gun his mom has for craft projects, we glue the pieces of string into each of the hot dogs till they look like sticks of dynamite, each with its own fuse.

We used to build these make-shift explosives back when we were in elementary school, pretending to demolish Lego cities we'd created. Now we plant the fake dynamite around his mom's container garden, making explosion noises as we imagine the clay pots blowing up

demolish

all over the yard. Sure, it's immature, but for an hour or so, our lives are simple and uncomplicated again.

BOOM!

Trouble on Wheels

The next day I fully intend to ignore Umberto but as soon as I sit down, he launches in.

launches

"Just to be clear," Umberto says. "I didn't copy your baby seals."

I know he's baiting me, yet I fall for it anyway. "Just like you didn't copy my monkey?"

"Exactly," he smirks. "What are the chances?"

"One in a billion." I know I should stop here but I don't. "About the same odds as you coming up with original material."

Umberto's eyes flash with anger. "You want to insult me, you better be prepared to back it up."

"Oh, I am."

"Good, then meet me behind the school at three o'clock. I'm going to kick your butt."

"WHAT?!" How did THAT just happen?

Before I can say anything else, Umberto takes off to the front of the room. It's not even eight thirty and the day's already heading for disaster.

If you don't count the time I stepped in the middle of Swifty and Tommy having it out last year, I've

preposterous

TAKE YOUR
MOM TO
THE PROM

dexterity

never been in a fight at school. Not to mention that I've never—nor do I know anyone else who has—been in a fight with a kid in a wheelchair. It's preposterous, and I look around to see if Umberto's kidding.

But the taunting expression is gone, replaced by eyes shooting daggers at me from across the room. He holds up three fingers. "Three o'clock—come feel the pain."

Is he insane? As Ms. McCoddle begins her lecture on Antarctica, a rising sense of dread fills my body. This is all a giant scare tactic, right? There's no way Umberto thinks I'm actually going to fight him... IN A WHEELCHAIR. I suddenly remember his dexterity with the lacrosse stick. Maybe Umberto's some upper-body martial arts expert who can't wait to practice his latest lethal move on Yours Truly. For the first time since summer, I actually feel myself sweat.

When the bell rings to switch classes, I race out the door.

"Umberto wants to fight me," I tell Matt.

"Yeah, right."

"I'm serious. At three, behind the school."

Matt tries to evaluate my expression to see if I'm pulling his leg.

evaluate

"You have to help me get out of it," I say.

"He's probably just kidding."

Swifty walks by on the way to his locker. "Three o'clock, huh? I can't wait to watch you go down."

"Great," Matt says. "Umberto probably told the whole school."

After I tell Swifty to get lost,

Carly comes up behind him. "You're not going to fight, are you?" she asks. "Please tell me you're not."

"And be called a chicken for the rest of the year?"

"Afraid to fight a kid in a wheelchair?" Matt adds. "You'll never hear the end of it."

The three of us look over to Umberto, surrounded by a cluster of our classmates. To think I wanted to help him, had even put together a plan to train Frank to be his helper. A sudden wave of self-righteousness sweeps over me. Who does this kid think he is, transferring to our school and stirring up trouble? Copying my comic strip, getting me in trouble with our teacher? Watching him now, I decide Umberto is the one who needs his butt kicked. Wheelchair or

self-righteousness

no wheelchair, I'm tired of this kid harassing me.

"Three o'clock," I tell Matt and Carly. "If Umberto wants a fight, he's going to get one."

I Hope You Know, This Means War

"You can't fight a kid in a wheelchair," Carly says. "It's just plain—what's the word?—*wrong*."

"For the millionth time, this wasn't my idea."

"It's Bullying Rule Number One," Carly pleads. "Just walk away."

interjects

"If I can't walk away, he can't either," Umberto interjects as he races down the hall.

"I have no intention of walking

away," I call after him. "I'll be there."

Carly grabs her books tighter to her chest and shakes her head sadly. "I want nothing to do with this. You're on your own."

I point up toward her locker, where Crash is waiting for her. "I don't think YOU'RE on your own."

She tilts her head, trying to decide whether or not to go to Crash. "I can't watch you do this," she says, then heads toward her boyfriend.

When the bell rings at the end of the day, Matt rubs my shoulders as if I'm a boxer going into the ring. I'm completely flabbergasted when we go outside and more than fifty kids are waiting.

"Fight, fight, fight!" everyone chants.

Part of me wants to run screaming

exhilarated

notoriety

through the double doors and not stop until I'm safely hidden underneath my bed at home. But another part of me is exhilarated by this sudden attention and notoriety. I look over and see Charlotte Mayo and Mackenzie Brennan chanting. I didn't even think they knew who I was.

"This is like an old-fashioned duel," Matt says. "It's awesome."

Billy Thompson, who lives a few houses down from Matt, chimes in. "Alexander Hamilton got killed in a duel."

"That's not going to happen today," Matt says.

My exhilaration suddenly shifts to fear, and I find myself with a serious case of flop sweat. "I've got to get out of here," I tell Matt. "Let's go."

"No one's going anywhere,"

Umberto says, wheeling up behind me. "Ready to get your butt kicked?"

As the other kids chant Umberto's name, I scan the school yard for a random teacher to put an end to the madness. Why isn't there ever an adult around when you need one?

random

"Pick your weapon," Umberto says. Across his lap, he's got two lacrosse sticks and two pairs of boxing gloves.

"Are you insane? Who brings boxing gloves to school?"

"I box at the YMCA," Umberto says. "I'm a black belt in karate, too."

Billy Thompson chimes in yet again. "Have you seen Umberto on YouTube breaking boards with his head? Or chopping a cinder block in half with his bare hands? He's amazing."

The person I now want to fight is Billy Thompson.

I turn to Matt. "This is ridiculous. I can't fight a kid in a wheelchair."

Umberto overhears me. "You want me to get out of my chair? Cuz I'll beat you lying on the ground too."

As my life flashes before my eyes, I think about my drawings and wish Super Frank were here to help me. He may be fictional, but no one else seems willing to help me out today.

"Enough stalling." Umberto tosses me a lacrosse stick. "You get on one end of the school yard, I'll get on the other. We'll meet in the middle and joust until one of us wins."

"You want to joust? What is this, medieval times?"

"Jousting began in Europe in the tenth century," Billy Thompson says. "It was first—"

medieval

"Will you please SHUT UP!" I yell.
I grab the lacrosse stick and head to
the other end of the yard. "Let's get
this over with."

Everyone starts chanting "Fight,
fight, fight" again, and when Stephen
waves his bandana, Umberto and I
race to the middle of the yard. Using
his wheelchair, he's much faster
than I am. Carly's words echo in
my head, reminding me what a
stupendously bad idea this is.

Before I get a chance to raise my
stick, Umberto smacks me in the
knee with his. As much as I try not
to react, it hurts, and I let out a
short scream. I hoist the lacrosse
stick above my head and get ready
to hit Umberto back when a shout
stops me in my tracks.

"Derek Fallon, put that stick down
now!"

bandana

reprimanded

disperse

defenseless

I'm embarrassed to be reprimanded by Ms. McCoddle, especially in front of half the school.

"I didn't even want to do this!" I say as the crowd begins to disperse. "This was all Umberto's idea."

Umberto has magically ditched the boxing gloves as well as his own lacrosse stick. I try to visualize the scene from Ms. McCoddle's perspective: me wielding a weapon at the defenseless new kid in a wheelchair who now wears an innocent expression.

"Both of you, principal's office, NOW!" she says.

I suddenly spot a crack in Umberto's calm demeanor. He seems as upset as I am.

"Ms. McCoddle, please—" I begin.

"We won't do it again," Umberto adds.

She spins around to face the two of us. "I'll give you two a choice: a one week detention with me or a meeting with Principal Demetri and your parents."

detention

Umberto and I answer in unison. "Detention."

"My classroom—let's go!"

All I can think of is what I'm going to tell my parents when I finally get home.

You Want Us to What?

Ms. McCoddle is still in super-serious mode as she erases the board in her room.

"Here's the plan: You two are going to collaborate on a project that's due next week."

I start to complain but think better of it. Umberto's back to wearing his cooperative grin. What a phony.

"Since you two are interested in

cooperative

comics, you can come up with one together—contributing without fighting."

"I'd love to collaborate, Ms. McCoddle," Umberto begins. "But it might be hard because Derek keeps taking all my ideas."

"ARE YOU OUT OF YOUR MIND?" Before the sentence is out of my mouth, I realize this was just a clever ploy to get me to blow my stack in front of our teacher. I compose myself before continuing.

ploy

"I think it's a great idea. It actually sounds fun," I say.

When Ms. McCoddle tries to hide a smile, I realize I've gone too far in the other direction. "Then it's settled. We start tomorrow. I want a note from both your parents saying they're on board."

Matt and Carly are waiting for

me by the school's front entrance. I don't bother looking behind me to see where Umberto's gone.

"Did you get in trouble?" Carly asks.

"Did she make you see Demetri?" Matt adds.

I tell them about detention, but what really makes them groan is the fact that I have to create a comic strip with Umberto as punishment.

"He doesn't have one original idea," Matt says. "All he does is copy your stuff."

Carly shakes her head, looking off into space. "I just don't get it. Why is he picking on you? You're such a nice kid."

I feel my cheeks flush at the unexpected compliment.

Behind Matt, I notice Umberto

still inside the school lobby. The automatic doors are locked, and he's trying to open the regular door and wheel himself through. No one else is around, and I'm the only one who can see him.

automatic

"Come on," I tell Matt and Carly. "Let's go."

Someone will probably come along to help Umberto. It's just not going to be me.

My First Detention

pestering

Needless to say, my parents are not happy when they find out I have a week's detention. My mother listens to my side of the story and says she'll call Ms. McCoddle tomorrow.

"It sounds like this new kid's really been pestering you. What do you think set him off?"

I tell her I've been trying to figure that out for weeks.

"We'll get to the bottom of this," she says. One of Mom's interns knocks at the door and says there's an emergency with a Dalmatian who got hit by a car. I feel bad about the dog but I'm I glad the conversation abruptly ends. I grab a handful of Girl Scout cookies and head to my room.

abruptly

I've got to hand it to Umberto— the guy's pretty ingenious when it comes to slipping out of trouble. It makes me wonder what he was like at his old school. Did he lure other innocent kids into detention there too?

ingenious

To take my mind off my punishment, I spend the rest of the afternoon working on my comic strip. I name the bad guy Roberto as a nod to my own school yard villain. I sketch him sitting in a jail cell with nothing but a cot, a toilet, and a giant cellmate covered in tattoos.

Drawing actually makes me feel better and by dinnertime I have a stack of papers full of Roberto in ridiculous situations and one new *Super Frank* comic strip.

As he serves the chicken, Dad says he wants to "throw his two cents in" by telling me to "take the high road" when kids are looking for trouble. His little talk has me wondering why parents have to resort to idioms when they want to have a serious discussion. It makes me want to "bury my head in the sand."

"So now that the dust has settled...," my mom begins.

I close my eyes. If she's starting

in with the idioms too, this can only mean they're gearing up for A Serious Conversation.

"We pulled together some information to go over with you," she continues.

"Information on what?" I ask.

My father looks me straight in the eyes. "Bullying."

Get Me Out of Here!

preoccupied

The last thing I want to do is spend even more time preoccupied with Umberto, but I can tell by both my parents' faces that there will be no escaping them tonight. They've even printed a handout from the Internet. I pray my dentist calls, demanding my presence for an emergency root canal.

"Bullying is a hot topic now," Dad

begins. "There are websites, books, and public service announcements where you can get a lot of information."

I'm almost embarrassed to ask the next question. "Are you telling me this because I'm being bullied or do you think I AM a bully because I got into a fight?"

My mother suddenly seems confused, a rarity for her. "From everything you've told me, Umberto's been bullying *you*. Am I wrong?"

rarity

"No! I just wanted to check." I'd give anything to change places with Frank in his cage right now. Anything.

My mother settles down. "The experts say when you're being taunted by a bully, the most important thing to do is walk away."

Both of them stare at me, waiting

relentless

for some kind of answer that makes sense.

"I know I should've walked away," I say. "I *tried* to. But Umberto was relentless."

"You still had a choice," my mother says. "You could've left school at three o'clock. You could've told a teacher."

"There are lots of things I could've done," I say. "But I didn't."

"Why?" It's the simplest of questions but not one with an easy answer.

My parents wait for me to respond. With this kind of patience, they'd probably make good surfers.

My mother finally tilts her head and meets my eyes. "I know why you went," she says. "I just want you to say it."

I know my parents well enough to know they're not going to let this subject die. It's the whole only-child thing: They have to over-analyze everything I do as if every tiny detail of my life is the most important thing in the world. I'm usually flattered by this kind of hyper-attention, but today it only wears me down.

I take a deep sigh. "I went because I didn't want to be the kid who was too afraid to fight a kid in a wheelchair."

"That's wrong on so many levels," she says. "First of all, even though he's in a wheelchair, Umberto could've beaten you by being smarter. Smart always counts in a fight."

I don't dare interrupt to find out

why my mother is suddenly an expert in the art of hand-to-hand combat.

"Second," she says. "If you thought you somehow deserved to win because you were able-bodied and he wasn't, that's wrong too."

I'm about to protest when she holds up her hand to stop me. "That's *your* part in all this. As far as Umberto goes, he needs to understand that being in a wheelchair isn't an excuse to be a bully. If he's using a physical challenge as an excuse for bad behavior, that's just as wrong."

Inquisition

I glance over at the clock, wondering when this Spanish Inquisition will finally end. My father must sense my discomfort because he takes a sheet of paper and slides it across the table.

discomfort

"Why don't you read this," he says. "Let us know what you think."

"Jeremy, I'm not really done," my mother says.

My father places his hand on hers. "I don't think we need to belabor the point."

belabor

At this moment, I love my father more than Christmas and my birthday combined. I love my mom too, but belaboring is what she lives for. When I look over at Frank, I swear he also breathes a sigh of relief.

I grab the paper and race to my room.

That was worse than a root canal and I've never even had one.

Some Crazy Facts

statistics

intimidation

Anyone who knows me knows I hate to read, but even I have to admit that some of the statistics on bullying and intimidation were interesting—and scary.

I shove the sheet in a folder and cram it under the books on my desk. Why did my parents give me such gloomy stuff to read before bed? I lie on the floor next to Bodi and try to pretend I'd never read it.

I appreciate my parents' efforts but Umberto shows no signs of stopping. I don't take much solace knowing that other kids around the world are being bullied much worse than I am. And I don't care what my mother says: The fact that Umberto is in a wheelchair does factor into it.

solace

The tips my parents have printed out run through my mind: avoid being alone with the bully, ignore his threats, walk away, find a safe place, tell a trusted adult. But when push comes to shove—literally—I don't know how helpful these tips will be. Maybe I'm being cynical, maybe these tips are foolproof and work every time. In the end, I decide I have nothing to lose by trying.

cynical

Let the Games Begin

Matt tells me he'll pull one of the fire alarms so he can get detention too but we know he won't do it. Carly is angry at both Umberto and me and decides to ignore him, which only makes Umberto try to get HER into trouble too. But Carly doesn't let herself get sucked into Umberto's evil plans.

Ms. McCoddle insists we suffer

through our punishment in her classroom instead of with Ms. Loughlin, who usually runs detention. Ms. McCoddle must know that Ms. Loughlin is always so focused on her knitting that kids can usually get away with pretty much anything while she's in charge. Instead, Ms. McCoddle grades papers in the front of the room while Umberto and I sit in our usual seats to begin our cartoon partnership.

We go through our own notebooks, ignoring each other for at least ten minutes before Ms. McCoddle interrupts the silence.

"If I don't have a comic you came up with TOGETHER by next week, detention will be extended to TWO weeks. Am I clear?"

Whatever happened to the happy,

extended

sing-songy kindergarten teacher Ms. McCoddle used to be? Umberto and I finally grunt out an acknowledgment and she turns back to her work.

"You think you have all the original ideas," Umberto says. "Why don't YOU start?"

"That's exactly why YOU should be the one to go first—to show you actually can create an original character on your own."

"That's easy," Umberto continues. "I could do it in my sleep."

"Then take a nap and come up with something." I put my arms behind my head as if I have all day.

It might be my imagination but it seems that Umberto's finally at a loss for words. He scans the room nervously.

"Come on," I taunt. "I'm waiting."

Umberto picks up his marker and

draws the first panel. My confidence falters a bit when I see that he doesn't need a ruler to make a crisp, straight line. He fills the first panel quickly and neatly, then pushes the paper across the desk.

falters

I stare at his artwork and then laugh. Ms. McCoddle looks up with a smile, probably thinking we're enjoying ourselves. Nothing could be further from the truth.

"You drew a penguin."

"No kidding," Umberto says. "If you're so good at animal identification, maybe you should be a zoologist."

zoologist

I hold up the paper and point to the wall behind me. "Now you're just copying from the bulletin board. I helped Ms. McCoddle put up that penguin myself."

Umberto leans back in his

wheelchair. "I didn't see that penguin. Your big head must've been blocking it."

"There are millions of animals on the planet, and you just happen to come up with a penguin?"

"What's the big deal? You came up with a baby seal." He smiles as he gestures toward the seals in the corner of the board.

"I came up with my baby seal character BEFORE this bulletin board went up."

basking

"Are you sure?" Umberto seems to really be basking in our argument. "Because I seem to remember this board being up first."

"You're lying!" I feel my cheeks flush, then watch as Ms. McCoddle rises from her desk.

"Is there a problem?" she asks.

"Umberto is copying someone else's ideas—AGAIN."

Umberto shrugs. "My colleague here isn't happy with the character I created. I was just trying to jump-start the creative process. I'm happy to try again if this one doesn't work for him."

Ms. McCoddle examines the drawing. I pray for her to hate it but she smiles instead. She holds the page up to me. "I think this penguin is endearing. Isn't this something you can work with, Derek?"

endearing

I want to tell her of COURSE I can work with a penguin. Who I CAN'T work with is Umberto. Instead I tell Ms. McCoddle I just have so many ideas I'm not sure which one to use first. She nods and returns to her desk.

"You stick your tongue out when you concentrate, do you know that?" Umberto asks. "I used to do that— back when I was two years old."

I ignore the insult and hand him the finished panel.

He studies the paper for a few moments. As much as I dislike Umberto, all I'm thinking while he's examining it is *Do you think it's good? Do you like it?* I hate myself for wanting his approval.

"A flamingo?" he finally says. "How are we supposed to create a comic strip about two birds who can't possibly exist in the same location?"

"Exactly," I answer.

Just like the two of us.

Detention Spy

monotonous

confinement

While waiting for Umberto at our next monotonous detention, I draw a cartoon about a prisoner of war in solitary confinement with nothing to entertain himself but bugs and leaves. I know I'm not the first kid in the history of the world to say this, but detention STINKS.

When Umberto wheels up to his desk, he doesn't seem as chipper as usual. If it were any other classmate, I'd ask what's wrong but because it's Umberto, I don't.

"Let's try to get a chunk of this done today," I suggest. "'Cuz I don't want our punishment to get extended."

"Oh, like I do," Umberto snaps.

He shoots me a look like I just punched his grandmother in the face.

"What's your problem?" Although I don't want to seem interested, curiosity has gotten the better of me.

Umberto rubs his left leg. "I've had a hard time sleeping, that's all. It's no big deal."

I watch him knead his leg the way my mom kneads dough when she bakes bread. "Does your leg hurt?"

knead

"I've kind of gotten used to it but last night was bad." He grabs the paper from my desk. "But not as bad as your lettering. Did you write this on a bus with no shock absorbers? While going down a hill?"

I grab the paper back and smooth it out on my desk. For a moment there I almost felt bad for Umberto. So much for being nice.

The two of us work on our strip, a story of two birds with nothing in common. When Ms. McCoddle comes over to check on our progress, she studies the panels carefully, then waits a few minutes before speaking.

"I'm not sure this is making any sense yet," she says slowly. "And it seems a little negative. Then again,

I'm not a cartoonist; you two are. I'm sure it'll come together in the end."

I'm glad our teacher is confident in our collaboration because I'm sure not. I take the opportunity to ask for permission to use the bathroom.

"You have five minutes before I come looking for you," Ms. McCoddle says.

The thought of Ms. McCoddle throwing open the door of the boys' room is enough for me to accelerate my pace down the hall. But I don't head toward the bathroom; I hurry to Mr. Owens's room to check on Matt's movie club.

accelerate

I stand on my toes and sneak a peek into the window of the door. I'm crestfallen when I see Matt in the front of the room laughing. The other kids are laughing too. My

crestfallen

materialized

worst fears have materialized: The rest of the world is having fun while I have detention.

As I'm about to head back to the classroom, I hear something and at first can't tell what it is. After a moment, I realize someone's crying. I look around the corner to find Carly leaning against her locker in tears. I look between Ms. McCoddle's classroom and Carly. Even with a five-minute deadline, I can't ignore one of my best friends.

"What's the matter?" I ask. "Are you okay?"

She cries harder when she sees me. "Crash just broke up with me."

"What? Why?"

She shrugs and wipes her tears with the edge of her sleeve. "I asked him but he wouldn't tell me."

From over my shoulder I hear Ms. McCoddle's voice. "Did I tell you I'd be looking for you, Derek?"

"I'll be right there."

"I'm counting to three," she says, as if I'm a baby who needs to be corralled back to his crib for naptime.

corralled

"I'm done at four if you can wait for me," I tell Carly. "Okay?"

She shakes her head. "I just want to go home."

"One . . . two . . ."

"I'm coming!" I race back to Ms. McCoddle's room. *Sheesh, get a life already.*

I slide into my seat, but the last thing I'm thinking about is working with Umberto. I haven't heard Carly cry since last year when Ginger the class hedgehog died while Carly was watching her. And I can't get the

devastated

image of her crying out of my mind; she looked so devastated.

I make it my mission to help Carly through this. As I put together a mental list of ways to take her mind off Crash, a tiny voice in my head becomes louder. And louder.

Carly's not going out with Crash anymore!

It may be bad news for Carly, but it's good news for me.

A Surprise from Umberto

When I ask Matt the next day about the comedy club, he insists it wasn't as much fun without me. "You should've seen Mr. Owens. He was furious when I told him we weren't doing romantic comedies. I think the guy had been prepping for weeks. He tried to shove his briefcase under his desk with his foot, but I know he brought in a pile of sappy DVDs."

sappy

waterlogged

When I tell Matt about seeing Carly yesterday, he's not surprised. "Crash is a waterlogged moron," he says. "It was only a matter of time before he blew it."

I nod in agreement but inside I'm thinking: *Carly's already had a relationship begin and end. Matt and I have no idea what she's going through.*

I texted Carly last night to see if she wanted to come over after I got back from detention today. She said yes, so I'm hoping Umberto and I can get through this afternoon's session without a lot of drama.

I tried to talk Ms. McCoddle out of detention, not because of Carly, but so I could run my cartoon club. I pulled out all the stops, telling her I was the one in charge and we were covering a ton of new stuff this week. She let me finish, then told me someone else would have to run the club since I'd still be in detention. It made me wonder if she and my mom took how-to-be-firm lessons at the same school.

When I finally get to my desk, I'm surprised to see Umberto looking at my photos of Bodi and Frank stuck inside my folder. I seize them from him.

seize

"I was just checking out your pets. Calm down."

"Stop going through my stuff!"

"Must be easier drawing a monkey with a real one around," Umberto continues. "You have a baby seal at home, too?"

As irritated as I am, I almost laugh at the image of a baby seal

satisfaction

sliding down the ice chute in our fridge but don't want to give Umberto the satisfaction of being funny. I'm surprised that what he really wants to talk about is my dog.

Umberto asks what kind of breed Bodi is and I tell him he's a mutt.

"Mine is too," he says. "A rescue dog."

It's never occurred to me that Umberto has a dog or any other pet. He rummages through his pocket for his cell and shows me a photo of himself sitting in a kitchen chair, feeding a small brown terrier on his lap.

"You're not supposed to feed dogs table scraps," I say. "My mom's a vet. I've heard her say it a million times."

Umberto shrugs. "Minnie loves

regular food. I sneak him bites all the time."

"Your dog is a male and you named him Minnie?" It's possibly the worst pet name I've ever heard, and given my mom's veterinary practice, that's saying a lot.

"I know. My grandmother named him. But he's a great dog. Walking him is usually the best part of my day."

It seems rude to ask Umberto the logistics of dog walking when he's in a wheelchair. Does the dog sit in his lap, run alongside him, pull Umberto by the leash? After a while I look at the clock and realize twenty minutes have gone by and Umberto and I haven't drawn a thing. Remembering that Carly's coming to my house after detention, I grab my markers and pad.

logistics

"Maybe we shouldn't have picked a penguin and a flamingo," I tell Umberto. "Should we start over with dogs? It might be easier."

He shakes his head. "I usually try really hard to finish a cartoon, even if it's difficult."

abandon

Umberto's work ethic makes me feel bad about how ready I was to abandon our new characters—until I realize how easy it is to keep working on a cartoon WHEN YOU START OFF BY COPYING SOMEONE ELSE'S. I turn to a clean sheet of paper and concentrate on creating a new panel.

After a few minutes, I push the paper across the desk. The penguin is sliding down a snowy hill and dive-bombing into the water. The flamingo stands on one leg on the shore, wearing an arctic fox like a fur coat. I'm embarrassed to admit how much I want Umberto to like it.

"It's funny," he says, "but wouldn't the arctic fox *eat* the flamingo?"

"In real life, sure. But this is a cartoon." Do I have to explain how coyotes don't really send away for weapons from the ACME Corporation to catch roadrunners? *Sheesh.*

"If we're bending the rules of animal behavior," Umberto says, "why don't we make the flamingo native to Antarctica while we're at it?"

"Because then it's not funny," I answer.

"Oh, is it funny now? I wasn't sure."

I snatch the panel back and ask Umberto what HE came up with. He shows me three panels drawn with precision. In the world of his perfect

precision

panels, the penguin and flamingo watch TV in an igloo.

"I don't get it," I say.

Umberto moves from side to side in his chair. "They're indoors because it's so cold."

"Yeah, but they're inside a house of ice."

"That's the *joke*! How can they be warm and cozy sitting in an igloo?"

We stare at each other blankly, neither of us willing to give an inch.

"But do you like how I drew the panels?" Umberto asks. "Or the lettering?"

unwilling

I shrug, unwilling to give him even that.

It looks like we're in for a mighty long detention.

Hanging with Carly

Carly knocks at the back door at exactly four thirty. The girl is so reliable, it's frightening.

"Cartoon club totally imploded without you," she says. "The twins knocked over every desk in the room, and when Susan tried to steal some makeup out of Ms. Ramirez's purse, they got into a huge screaming match."

"WHAT?"

"Calm down. I was kidding. Matt and I ran it together. It was totally fine."

"Glad to see you're back to your old self."

But when she smiles, I catch a glimpse of some of the sadness I saw in her eyes yesterday.

My mother is happy to have Carly stay for dinner. Half the reason Carly and I started hanging out in the first place is that our moms are friends. Mom gives Carly a hug, which is kind of okay yet embarrassing at the same time.

The first thing we decide to do is take Bodi to the dog park. My mom asks if we can bring Snickers along, and when Carly sees how cute the puppy is, she's happy to oblige.

oblige

The dog park is usually a nice walk—seven blocks away—but for some reason three car alarms go off, so the leisurely stroll ends up sounding like a wartime air raid. I tell Carly how Ms. McCoddle's idea of getting Umberto and me to collaborate on a comic strip is the worst idea in the history of bad ideas.

leisurely

Not only does our comic stink but our relationship—if you can call it that—is as combative as ever. (I forget to mention how incredible Umberto's lettering and panels are.) As I talk, I realize all this conversation about Umberto will probably mean that Carly will want to discuss Crash. As torturous as that sounds, it's one of the reasons I invited her over today. When she starts to talk about

combative

how hard it is to see Crash in the hall now, I nod politely and try to be a good friend.

At the dog park, I unlock the fence slowly, making sure there aren't any gigantic or mean-looking dogs who might injure Snickers or Bodi. When we take the dogs off their leashes, Bodi happily frolics through the mulch after Snickers. Carly's probably the only girl I know who's not embarrassed to pick up dog poop in a plastic bag in front of a classmate. It probably doesn't sound like much of an endorsement, but in my book it's high praise. Maybe I can talk her into helping me with Frank's daily maintenance too.

We sit on one of the benches and imitate a woman on the other side of the park talking to her collie.

frolics

endorsement

Carly and I laugh hysterically as we try to duplicate the woman's thick Scottish accent.

duplicate

Mr. Danson is there with his greyhound, but poor Bodi can barely keep up with Murphy today. He chases the dog for a lap, then settles under the bench I'm sitting on.

Carly is vibrant at dinner, telling my parents about her mom's landscaping business and a pesky mole that's been terrorizing one of her mom's clients. I have to concentrate to keep my manners in check; Carly waits patiently to swallow before she talks and puts her fork down between bites. It's almost as if she actually listened when her parents were trying to teach her dining etiquette.

vibrant

Even when Carly was little, I

etiquette

doubt she was the kind of girl who'd want to dress Frank up in doll clothes or have a monkey tea party, so I'm not surprised when what she wants to do after dinner is help me get Frank ready for monkey college. I let her watch a segment from the training DVD before we take Frank out of his cage.

segment

I demonstrate how Frank can now open a DVD case on his own. Like the trainers on the video, I reward Frank with lots of praise when he accomplishes the task.

"Let's teach him how to pick up something that's been dropped," Carly says. "Like a remote."

For the next hour, we take turns sitting on one of the kitchen chairs dropping the TV remote, coaxing Frank to pick it up. A few times the batteries fall out when the remote hits the floor, and it doesn't seem as if Frank and Bodi appreciate the noise. We move Operation Teach Frank into the den to safeguard the remote and Bodi's sanity. Carly asks me for paper and keeps meticulous notes of our results—something I've never done in all the training I've conducted. It's just one more reason why Carly's the smartest kid I know.

safeguard

meticulous

On the forty-third drop, Frank tentatively picks up the remote from the rug and hands it back to me. Carly and I rejoice at this new step in Frank's education, praising him as if he's just won a gold medal.

tentatively

As Carly and I have a celebratory snack of pears and lemonade, I can't help but remember when Matt and I had a big fight earlier this year. Carly came over to take my mind off the fact that I was at war with my best friend. Her friendship really helped. Based on how much fun we had today, I hope my reciprocal effort works for her, too.

"This was great," she says when her mom comes to pick her up. "Can I help you train Frank again?"

I tell her of course. For most of the time we were together, neither of us mentioned Crash or Umberto. That's probably why we had so much fun. Sometimes sticking your head in the sand isn't a bad thing after all.

I Give My Brain
a Rest

Saturday, I try not to fixate on detention and invite Matt over to help me rummage through the garage for Old Stuff We Forgot About That We Can Still Play With. In fact, our garage is so full of that kind of junk, we've never been able to park a car there.

Because my mom's having lunch with one of her friends and my dad's on deadline, no one stops us when

Matt and I carry Frank's cage out to the garage. I bring Bodi's dog bed so he can join us too.

unbearable

"You better finish that cartoon with Umberto. Two weeks' detention would be unbearable." Matt holds up a broken weed wacker we could still take apart and build something with.

"Don't worry—I'll finish that cartoon if I have to do the whole thing myself."

"I guess that wouldn't be much of a collaboration."

I can barely hear him since Matt is wearing the huge rubber Frankenstein mask my father used to wear on Halloween when I was little.

"Why does my mom keep all this stuff?" I point to the tower of cardboard boxes in the corner of the garage.

"We can make another robot," Matt suggests.

"The last time we got silver paint all over my dad's bike, remember?"

"It totally blended in. I can't believe he noticed," Matt says.

I hold up a sturdy box that had probably held a pair of my father's shoes. "Or we could put on one of our legendary magic shows."

legendary

Matt drops the hose. "Should we bring back the Great Mattini?"

"And the Amazing Derek?"

We hightail it to the back of the garage, where my mother keeps two plastic tubs of fabric she never uses. I guess somewhere in my mom's mind she imagines having all this spare time to sew; in reality, she barely has five minutes to sew a button on a shirt, never mind make an outfit from scratch. If she knew

hightail

how often Matt and I have used her material as parachutes, capes, and blankets for Bodi, she wouldn't be happy.

Matt grabs a long piece of silky purple fabric; I choose a black piece with splashes of green. We drape them over us like magical robes. I hate it when people dress up their dogs in little raincoats and tutus, but I don't want Bodi to miss out on the fun. I rummage through the box until I find a small piece of sparkly fabric to wrap around him, then run inside to grab some safety pins. When I come back, Matt's wrapped some striped fabric in a turban around his head. He hands me some paisley material for mine.

paisley

"Frank looks left out," Matt says.

"What are you talking about?

He's the main attraction." I find the scissors and start cutting holes in the shoebox.

Matt immediately sees where I'm going with this and scans the garage for more props. He comes up with fake spiderwebs and a lantern we use for camping. We clear off the table in the middle of the floor and cover it with a deep blue piece of fabric. Then we set up the spider-webs and turn off the garage light for effect.

"Wait, wait!" I run inside and find an old CD player and put on a scratched CD of spooky sounds my mom used to play from the porch when kids came to trick-or-treat.

"Don't make it look too much like a haunted house," Matt says. "We're magicians, remember?"

supernatural

squawk

delicately

"Magicians with supernatural powers," I remind him.

I take Frank out of his cage and carefully place him in the large shoebox.

"You think he'll squawk when you put his head in the hole?" Matt asks.

"Not if I do it right. Hopefully he'll think it's a little bed." I place Frank's head through the hole, then put his feet through the hole in the other end. I do everything so delicately that Frank doesn't freak out.

I replace the cover. Frank now looks like a perfect assistant lying onstage in a magic box. Matt takes a photo with his phone while I go to the workbench on the back wall and find my dad's old saw.

"Just to check that we're on the same page," Matt says, "we're only *pretending* to cut Frank in half, right?"

"No, we're really going to do it," I answer. "Why are you even ASKING me that?"

We pose for a photo on Matt's phone. I hold up Frank-in-the-Box, and Matt picks up Bodi and puts him on the table. When we look at the photo, we see our turbans are falling off our heads, so we adjust them before beginning the show.

"Ladies and gentlemen!" Matt begins. "I am the Great Mattini, and this fine fellow beside me is the Amazing Derek."

I take a low bow, still holding Frank so he doesn't escape. Matt waves the saw in the air.

"For tonight's astounding act, the Amazing Derek will saw a live monkey in half!"

astounding

hoax

ceremoniously

I realize our pretend-audience should actually see us put Frank in the box to know it's not some kind of hoax. I take Frank out of his magic box and put him back in again.

It seems as if Bodi wants to participate a little more, so I find an old party hat and slip it over his head. Matt holds the saw ceremoniously, bending it for effect.

"And now, right before your very eyes," he continues, "the Amazing Derek will begin this death-defying act."

But when I raise the saw above the box, I am looking straight into the eyes of my parents standing in the driveway. My mother's carrying a doggy bag from her favorite restaurant; she is NOT happy. My father, on the other hand, is holding his hand up to his face and looks like he's trying not to laugh.

My mother wordlessly walks over to the table and takes Frank out of the shoebox. The CD is now skipping, stuck on a morbid sound of someone wailing.

morbid

"Um, you know we weren't really going to saw him in half," I say meekly.

meekly

Mom removes the party hat from Bodi's head and unfastens the safety pin, letting his sparkly outfit fall to the floor. Matt and I take off our turbans and capes. Then she extends her arms for the fabric, which we carefully hand over. My father shoots me an expression that says Don't Even Think About Talking, and for once I'm smart enough to take his advice. The music continues

varieties

to wail over and over until I finally punch the STOP button.

Out of all the varieties of MomMad, silent MomMad is by far the worst. Mom puts Frank inside his cage and brings it inside. My father—also smart enough not to argue with her when she's like this—takes Bodi inside too.

"I hate to take off—" Matt begins.

"Are you kidding? I wish I could leave too. Get out and don't look back."

Matt doesn't need any convincing; he jumps on his skateboard and heads home.

I go inside and see my mother examining Frank to make sure he's okay. Then she checks his diaper and hands him to me.

I head to her office, incredibly

relieved. ANYTHING is better than Mom's silent treatment, including changing a monkey's poopy diaper.

It's going to be a very long Saturday.

NO!

grudge

Carly still surfs with Heinz on Saturdays, which means seeing Crash whether she wants to or not. After yesterday's fiasco with the magic show, I still beg my parents for money for another surf lesson, not just because I want to surf again but to make sure Carly's okay. One good thing about my mom—she doesn't hold a grudge. I'm filled with gratitude that she gives me money without a lecture. Then she does even better by driving us to Santa Monica. I fall off the board less frequently than before and end up riding a few small waves all the way in. It turns out Crash didn't show up. Who knows, maybe he's embarrassed about seeing Carly too.

gratitude

After we get back from the beach, I ask Carly if she wants to come over, but I think all that worrying about running into Crash took a lot out of her and she just wants to stay at home. I change Frank when I get in, then work with him on picking up the dropped remote again. He's slowly getting the hang of it, just the way I have with my drawing—practicing again and again.

Bodi needs some time too and

wags his tail the whole way to the dog park. Mr. Danson and Murphy aren't there but two Labs chase a soggy tennis ball and Bodi cheerfully tags along behind them. I'm in a good mood—until I spot someone approaching from the other side of the park. In a wheelchair. I don't say anything, hoping this is just a bully mirage and the image of Umberto will dissipate soon.

dissipate

"What are YOU doing here?" I ask Umberto when we meet. Is this guy trying to wreck my weekends too?

maneuvers

Umberto maneuvers his chair through the mulch and woodchips. "My aunt lives down the street. I thought I'd let Minnie run around while we visit." He points to a small brown terrier following two pugs. I have to admit Minnie is cute. Not that I'd tell Umberto.

"Is that your dog?" he asks. "I recognize him from the picture."

Umberto points to Bodi, who's sniffing the butt of a giant Great Dane. I'm grateful Umberto doesn't turn my dog's idea of fun into a joke.

"Hey, we have to finish that comic for Ms. McCoddle or we're looking at more detention," Umberto says. "That's the last thing I want."

"Oh, like I do." My sarcasm is lost on Umberto, who starts to wheel toward Bodi.

"Is your dog okay?"

I turn around and see Bodi across the park, lying on the ground. When I run to him, the two Labs think I want to play and chase after me.

Bodi's breathing heavily and his legs are moving as if he's running, which scares me more than if he were just lying there. I look around for help, but besides Umberto there's only a woman with a headset, yakking on the phone and throwing tennis balls to the Labs. I have to get Bodi to my mom's office. Fast.

latched

I pick up Bodi and run toward the dog park gate. It's a latched system of double doors so the animals can't escape. I wonder how I'm going to open them. To my surprise, Umberto's already there with Minnie in his lap. But the latch is up high and he can't reach it.

"Hey, you!" Umberto shouts to the woman on the phone. "A little help here!"

The woman sees Umberto in his

wheelchair and me carrying Bodi and hurries over to unlatch the heavy metal gate. I look down at Bodi and try to decide what's wrong. I'm not a vet like my mom but my guess is that he's having some kind of seizure. I want to ask the woman for a ride to my house but I've never seen her before and she's engrossed in her phone call again. I run as fast as I can while carrying a sixty-pound dog but I'm not moving fast enough.

engrossed

"We can go to my aunt's," Umberto says. "It's right down the street."

"My mom's a vet, remember? I'm going home."

Umberto moves Minnie to the side of his chair. "Give me your dog."

"What are you talking about?"

"I don't know how far you have to go but you'll definitely get there faster if you can run. Give me Bodi. Come on!"

intentions

When Umberto holds out his gloved hands, there isn't time to analyze his intentions. All I can think about now is saving Bodi's life. I place my beloved dog in Umberto's lap, then grab the handles of his wheelchair.

"Run!" Umberto says. "As fast as you can. Don't worry about me."

I don't tell him he's not the one I'm worried about. I race the seven blocks as fast as I can. Since most of the sidewalks are old and haven't been redone for people in wheelchairs, we have to run in the street. I look down to check on Bodi. He's now lying quietly in Umberto's arms. I just hope he's still breathing.

"Truck on the left!" Umberto yells. I swerve the wheelchair to the right, up a sidewalk ramp—finally—that leads to the top of my street.

swerve

I race the three blocks to my road, praying my mom's home. I push the wheelchair up the steep hill of my driveway—good to go down on skateboards, not so good for shoving wheelchairs—and screech to a halt outside the back door. I hurry into the kitchen, leaving Bodi momentarily with Umberto.

momentarily

"Mom!" I yell. "It's Bodi!"

My mom grabs her glasses from the counter and hurries outside. She nods to Umberto and gently takes Bodi. As I follow her into her office on the other side of the driveway, I realize Umberto's still in his chair by the kitchen door.

I grasp the handles of his wheelchair and lift him backward up the three steps to my mother's office, praying we got here in time.

Please Be Okay

My mother works quietly and efficiently as she checks Bodi. I have a zillion questions but I know enough not to bother her while she's performing an examination.

examination

Umberto seems to take the whole thing in, watching my mother as she inspects Bodi's tongue and eyes.

"Looks like he had a seizure," she

says. "It's too soon to see if there'll be permanent damage."

She leans in close to Bodi and pets him tenderly. It's not just because he's our dog—I've seen her do this to all her animal patients.

"Is he going to be okay?" Umberto asks.

"We'll need to keep our eye on him," Mom answers. "But hopefully, yes."

In all the commotion, I realize I haven't introduced my mother to Umberto. I can tell from her expression she just figured out Umberto must be the kid who's been terrorizing me. She's too gracious to say anything now, but I know she'll grill me for information the second Umberto leaves.

gracious

"Sometimes animals go into shock afterward," my mom says.

"It's a good thing you got him here quickly."

I tell my mom the only reason we got here so fast is that Umberto let us use his wheels.

"There are only a few benefits to being in a wheelchair, and racing at top speed is one of them," Umberto says with a smile.

Bodi seems to be okay, resting on the carpet. I wait until my mother leaves the room before I ask Umberto why he helped me.

He looks at me as if the answer is obvious. "Like I'm going to sit there and watch a dog die. What kind of obnoxious creep do you think I am?"

obnoxious

I don't answer the question. After a few minutes Umberto starts laughing.

"Okay, maybe I *have* ranked

pretty high on the obnoxious scale. But doing nothing while an animal's in distress? That's not me."

My mother hands us two bottles of water and a container of chocolate-covered almonds from the office kitchen. She also feeds Minnie a dog biscuit on her way back to the house. Minnie has a field day sniffing around the many pet smells in the waiting room. I pet him for a few minutes so he doesn't feel threatened.

Underneath the shock and upset of this chaotic day, something nags at me. I take a large gulp of water before asking the question I've wondered about for a long time. "Why have you been such a jerk to me?"

Umberto shrugs, which makes

chaotic

me feel angry all over again, as if this afternoon never happened. "Don't take it personally," he finally says.

"It's hard not to take it personally when you've made a mission out of bullying me."

"Wow. You think I'm a bully? Really?" Umberto actually seems surprised.

"What would YOU call it?"

Umberto's tone is now apologetic. "I guess I have been. I'm really sorry."

I wait for him to say more, and after a few moments, he does. "I got picked on a lot at my last school. I definitely didn't want to come here and turn into one of those jerks who tortures other kids in his class."

"Well, you did."

He nods in agreement. "Maybe I was just nervous about being new and having to start from scratch in the friend department."

I try to make sense of what he's saying, but it's hard. "If you were anxious about making friends, wouldn't it be easier to be NICE?"

Umberto looks at me, then bursts out laughing. "I guess I'm not used to doing things the easy way."

"Obviously." I start laughing too. "I mean, we had drawing in common. And cartoons!"

We finish the rest of the chocolate-covered almonds and head back outside. I carry Bodi and hold open the door with my hip. My parents suddenly appear out of nowhere as if waiting to pounce.

pounce

I introduce Umberto to my dad, who shakes his hand, then gets behind his chair, helping Umberto down the steps to the driveway with Minnie tagging along behind.

"I'm sorry there's no handicap access," Dad apologizes.

My mom explains she's been saving up to renovate and points to the side of the building where a ramp will lead to her office. She's being nice, but not overly nice, and I know it's because of how mean Umberto's been to me. But now he's the reason my dog is still alive and I'm ready to forgive and forget.

renovate

My father lifts Umberto's wheelchair up the steps to our kitchen while I carry Bodi. Umberto's face lights up when he sees my monkey. "Live and in person, it's Super Frank!"

I take Frank out of his cage and gently hold him toward Umberto.

Minnie isn't as excited as Umberto to meet Frank and begins to bark. Umberto reaches down and picks Minnie up to safety in his lap. I tell Umberto I'd like to show him what Frank can do.

navigate

Thankfully, our doorways are wide enough for Umberto to navigate. He follows me to the den, where I demonstrate Frank's skills with opening and retrieving DVDs. When I show him the monkey college DVD, Umberto watches in amazement.

"I KNEW you'd think this was cool," I say. "I wanted to show you this the first day we met."

"I was stupid," Umberto admits. "And I'm really sorry."

I keep checking on Bodi, who still seems tired. I don't want to think about how close I came to losing him today.

After a while, I go upstairs and bring down my markers and several pads. Umberto and I spend the rest of the afternoon doing what we should've done from Day One— making each other laugh with our drawings.

You're Friends
with WHO?

Throughout the day, I violate school policy and text my mother a thousand times to check on Bodi. She tells me he's fine and to get back to class. Both Carly and Matt are concerned about Bodi and shocked that Umberto was the one who helped save him.

As expected, the word *skeptical* doesn't begin to describe Matt and

skeptical

Carly when I tell them Umberto and I hung out at my house for the rest of the day.

"You got detention because of him!" Carly says.

"He totally copied your cartoons," Matt adds. "He gave you a stupid nickname."

"We kind of had fun," I say defensively.

Carly remains doubtful. "Suppose this is all some fiendish plot to get your guard down so he can ambush you when you least expect it?"

ambush

"He's probably got some complicated evil plan, just waiting for the perfect time to annihilate you." Even though it's his idea, Matt shudders at the thought.

annihilate

I smile because I know if the tables were turned, I'd be saying the same things. Carly and Matt are good friends, and I can't blame them for not trusting Umberto. All I can tell them is that Umberto helped me save Bodi, and right now that's good enough for me. After much persuading, Matt and Carly decide to give Umberto a chance, while still keeping their eyes out for trouble.

Truth be told, I didn't trust Umberto 100 percent either. After he left my house, my parents OF COURSE wanted to dissect everything that happened. I'm not kidding when I say I'd sooner sign up for another week of detention than sit through one more parental interrogation.

dissect

But today Umberto's been making an effort to be a regular friend. He doesn't call me names or egg me on to fight him. He shows me new cartoons he did last night starring a neatly drawn octopus. I compliment him on the strip's quirky point of view.

quirky

"Why did you put so much effort into copying my strips if you had original ideas all along?"

I detect the old, devilish Umberto when he starts to laugh. "I don't know. Maybe because I knew it would drive you crazy."

His answer isn't rational and doesn't help me understand the events of the past month. I chalk it up to THINGS PEOPLE DO THAT DON'T MAKE SENSE and race out the door to see Bodi as soon as the bell rings.

"Hold on a second!" Ms. McCoddle says.

"But my dog—"

"Your dog can wait." She holds out her hand. "Either I get your collaboration today or you're both here another week."

"Ask and you shall receive." Umberto practically skids across the room, sliding up next to Ms. McCoddle. "Check out the lettering. It's impeccable."

impeccable

Ms. McCoddle lays the sheets of paper Umberto and I finished at my house yesterday across her desk. A slow smile creeps across her face. "Not bad, boys. Not bad at all."

"Does that mean detention is hereby revoked?" I ask.

revoked

She almost tousles my hair the way she used to back in kindergarten but thankfully stops herself. She gestures toward the door. "The two of you—go!"

I race Umberto to the front door of the school.

He beats me by a good ten seconds.

Matt Joins In

After a few days of Umberto being nice, Matt surprises me by asking Umberto if he wants to come over to his house and hang out with us after school. Umberto asks Bill, the van's driver, if he can drop us all off at Matt's. Bill thinks about it for a moment, then says okay. We watch Umberto guide his wheelchair into the van's lift. I realize how much I take for granted just jumping into the car with my mom to get around the city. Matt gives the driver his address, and we settle into the extra seats.

While Umberto talks to Bill about last night's Lakers game, I lean over to Matt. "I thought we were going skateboarding."

"We are," he answers.

Matt's plan suddenly dawns on me, and I break into a huge grin. "Are you thinking what I'm thinking?"

"I bet that chair can go really fast," Matt says.

When we look up, Umberto is watching us. "I'll put my wheels up against yours anytime," he says.

"You don't stand a chance," I answer.

Bill says he'll go out for a coffee and pick Umberto up in an hour; Umberto calls his mom to say he'll be a little late. The three of us grab helmets from Matt's overstuffed garage and head to the hill at the top of his street.

I don't want to be a spoilsport but looking at the steepness of the hill suddenly fills me with worry.

spoilsport

"Are you sure this is okay?" I ask Umberto.

"There are kids who take customized chairs into the skate park in Venice," Umberto says. "And that thing's a bowl."

customized

Matt shrugs, not worried in the least. "Are you using your arms or not?" he asks Umberto.

"I don't know," Umberto answers. "Will you be using your legs?" And before I can even yell GO, Umberto is rolling down the hill.

Matt and I take off after him on our boards.

Umberto beats us, but not by much. We take turns pushing Umberto back up the hill. Matt and I slalom around Umberto's wheelchair as we take another run.

As we head to the van later, both Matt and I have to admit being with Umberto pushed us to ride as fast as we ever have.

mobility

"Just because my mobility is impaired doesn't mean I can't kick your butts," Umberto gloats. "You should see me play basketball."

We grab ice pops from the freezer and sit on the curb waiting for Bill's van. I gather up the courage to ask Umberto about his physical challenges.

"I have a spinal birth defect," he says. "I got used to being in a chair a long time ago."

"That stinks," I say.

Matt nods in agreement.

Umberto shrugs. "That's just the way it is."

There's no arguing with Umberto on that, but his honesty and grace make me like him even more.

When Bill pulls up, Umberto gets in the van and waves good-bye.

As we watch the van drive away, Matt reaches down for his board. "I like him," he says. "And he's certainly fast in that chair. But I'm still not sure I trust him."

I understand Matt's feelings, but I also know that friendships don't work without trust and I don't want to be the person to sabotage a potentially good one. So I decide to put my faith in Umberto and see what happens.

sabotage

My Best Idea,
Hands Down

Bodi's on the mend from his seizure
and I can finally relax. My mother
has the Bodi Is Getting Old
conversation with me at dinner,
which makes me start to cry into
my fried rice. I know Bodi's old, I
know this was a close call, but can I
just enjoy Bodi a little while longer?
Sheesh, Mom. Let me eat in peace.

After hanging out with Umberto

for a few weeks, I come to appreciate some of his good qualities. Despite all the evidence when we first met, it turns out Umberto takes his friendships seriously, almost as much as Carly and Matt do. He helps me with our English assignments and recommends books at my reading level that don't seem babyish. He even gives me tips on my lettering. In exchange, I give him some pointers I've learned from Dad and let him come over to sketch Dad's mannequins.

evidence

But my most innovative idea comes while Matt and I take a surfing lesson with Heinz. As he finds us boards and booties in his messy truck, I scan some brochures shoved in a box behind the driver's seat. And just like that, I get an amazing

innovative

idea. (Turns out my last one—training Frank to be Umberto's companion—wasn't a great idea after all. Umberto did enjoy meeting Frank but admitted he wouldn't want a capuchin for a helper. I guess monkey companions aren't for everyone.)

$$S = \frac{1}{6}k\,(\Delta t)^3$$
$$- k\,(\Delta^2 + 2v)$$
$$\times y_1 - y_2\,(t-4)$$
$$S_{arc} + 4v + y^2$$

complex

My new idea is a thousand times better, taking several weeks to put into action. The plan is so complex, I even have to run it by Umberto's mother when I meet her at his house one Sunday afternoon. Her eyes light up when I tell her what I have in mind. She tells me to count her in, which I take as a sign that this idea might actually be one of my better ones.

As expected, Carly has a million suggestions, most of which are excellent.

* * *

On the day of Operation Umberto, Carly, Matt, and I watch the van drive down Bay Street in Santa Monica. Umberto's mom, his brother Eduardo, and Bill wait as Umberto's chair lowers to the pavement.

"What is this?" Umberto asks. "Some kind of surprise party?"

"You could say that." I get behind his chair and push him toward the parking lot, where Heinz wears his perpetual grin and wetsuit. He rummages through his truck and throws Umberto a suit.

perpetual

Umberto looks up, confused.

"If you're going surfing, you need a wetsuit. That water's cold," Heinz says.

Umberto still can't understand what's going on.

I hold out one of Heinz's brochures

from Access Sports. On the cover, there's a photo of Heinz surfing with a kid with physical challenges on the front of his board.

Umberto seems afraid. "I can't do this," he says. "What if I fall off? I can't swim, never mind surf!"

"Heinz will be out there with you," I say. "Plus, you'll have this." I toss him a life jacket from Heinz's truck.

Umberto holds up the wetsuit. "I'm not even sure I can get this on."

Heinz, Matt, and I surround Umberto's wheelchair and hold up beach towels, making a privacy screen for him to change behind.

"It's like putting on a pair of pants at home," Eduardo says. "Two seconds, come on."

Carly and Umberto's mother move to the front of the truck while

Matt, Heinz, and I keep our towels up until Eduardo whisks them down like a magician. Umberto sits in his chair, wearing the wetsuit.

He grins from ear to ear until he looks toward the water and the large expanse of sand. "My chair's not going to go on that. You guys will have to carry me."

expanse

"Who do you think you are, Cleopatra?" his brother asks. "You'll have to get yourself down there."

"In this." Carly comes around from the front of the truck pushing a wheelchair with giant yellow wheels as thick as tire tubes.

Eduardo helps guide Umberto from his regular chair into the new one.

"We use these at Access Sports," Heinz says. "They're not fast, but you can definitely ride on the beach."

Umberto's already out of the parking lot, cruising down the boardwalk. When I catch a glimpse of his mother, I see she has tears in her eyes. When she notices me looking at her, she wipes her cheeks with her hands. "Umberto hasn't been to the ocean in years," she says. "He used to love the beach as a baby."

The new wheelchair gets stuck a few times, but Umberto manages to keep going. Like some kind of beach procession, the rest of us follow him down to the water's edge. Heinz has him sit forward in the chair while he adjusts the life jacket.

procession

Heinz explains they're going to paddle out together on his longboard. "We'll wait for just the right wave, then I'm going to stand on the back of the board and you're going to lie across the front."

"Like a boogie board," Carly interjects.

"If you fall off, don't worry—the vest will keep you afloat, and I'll be right there to grab you." It's obvious Heinz is not just some crazy hippie surfer but someone who spends time sharing his passion with others physically less able. It makes me see what Carly's liked about her instructor all along.

passion

While we're getting ready for Umberto to go out, I notice Carly scanning the waves. I don't have to ask who she's looking for. She blushes when she spots me.

"He already has another girl-friend," she says.

"She's probably not half as great

good-natured

as you are." Before the sentence leaves my mouth, I already regret it, especially with Matt so close by to tease me.

Carly gives me a good-natured punch in the arm. "Thanks for trying to make me feel better." She picks up her board and heads into the water behind Heinz and Umberto.

Matt and I stand on the shore and watch Heinz guiding the board out as Umberto paddles through the waves.

"He's got amazing upper-body strength from being in that chair," Eduardo says. "I bet he's not even sore tomorrow."

Umberto's mother seems happy and nervous at the same time. When a large wave sneaks up on them, Umberto almost gets knocked off but Heinz holds the board firmly and Umberto stays on. Umberto's mom grabs Eduardo's arm; he pats her reassuringly.

reassuringly

"Heinz is amazing in the water," I tell her. "He's been surfing his whole life. You'll see."

We watch Heinz gracefully climb onto the board without upsetting Umberto. Carly sits on her board nearby, the three of them chatting as they wait for just the right wave. I no longer regret telling Carly how great she is. Looking at her now, drenched in sunshine and saltwater, she seems about as perfect as a girl can be.

gracefully

drenched

"They're going to grab that next one," Matt says. "You just watch."

In the few times Matt and I have been surfing, he's been better at reading the waves. I pretty much just go along with what Heinz says but Matt has a real feel for it. Sure enough, Heinz and Carly start shouting to Umberto to paddle.

And paddle he does—furiously, with all the power of that octopus he drew in his comic strip. Heinz pops up and steers the board with his body, leaning left, carving his way expertly across the wave. We all hear an elated Umberto yell like Tarzan as he rides in.

elated

Matt, Eduardo, and I run into the water to greet Umberto as Heinz hops off the board. Umberto's mom follows behind us, not even taking the time to remove her straw sandals.

"You were amazing!" I say.

"You should've seen your face!" Matt adds.

After checking that he really is okay, Umberto's mother and brother step back so Heinz can guide the board out to the waves. The four of us stand knee-deep in the water and watch Carly ride her own wave to shore.

Umberto and Heinz catch six more rides before it's time for us to head back.

"Dude!" Umberto says to me, now sounding like Heinz. "This was the greatest day of my life."

"It was a team effort." I gesture to Carly, Matt, Heinz, Bill, Eduardo, and Umberto's mom.

Umberto changes back into his clothes and continues to talk to me through our makeshift terry-cloth barricade. "I am TOTALLY signing up for surf camp next summer," he says.

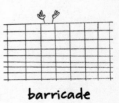

barricade

Eduardo patiently helps Umberto into his wheelchair. As Bill drives off with the family, Umberto waves from the window, looking like the happiest kid on the planet.

I reach into my pack for water bottles and an envelope for Heinz. It's money from my last birthday, plus a donation from my parents to cover the cost of his time and equipment.

donation

Heinz shakes his head and refuses the payment. "I borrowed the equipment from friends, so no worries. Besides, I enjoyed today as much as Umberto did. Save it for another time when we can all ride some waves together."

And that's exactly what we do.

A Cartoonist's Real Job

Umberto can't stop talking about surfing, about Heinz, and how perfect the waves are in Santa Monica. He constantly checks Surfline, keeping track of conditions even on days he has no way of getting to the beach. His comics reflect his new passion with a Ketchup Bottle Surfer as his main character. (No one can ever accuse Umberto of being subtle.)

subtle

One afternoon, I ran into Crash at the skateboard shop while shopping for a new board with my dad. When Crash waved without speaking from across the store, I decided to go over and talk to him.

Maybe it was my new confidence from working through all the weird stuff with Umberto that made it a little less awkward to approach him. We talked about boards, about Heinz, but never mentioned Carly, which was probably just as well. Crash seemed more like the kid who helped the woman in my mom's waiting room that day than the guy who dumped one of my best friends. Spending time with Crash—if only for a few minutes—made me feel a bit better belittling him all those times with Matt.

Cartoon club ends, as does Matt's comedy class. (Mr. Owens seems more upset about it than Matt does.) So with some extra time on my hands, I decide to make a new comic strip. This one doesn't showcase a monkey with super powers or a criminal baby seal, but a quiet mutt and a noisy boy. Sure, if you substitute a stuffed tiger for the dog it's a bit like *Calvin and Hobbes* but even if I draw every day for the rest of my life I could never hope to come up with anything half as good as that.

The boy in my cartoon is not as mischievous as Calvin and the dog is definitely calmer than Hobbes. The strip is called *Man's Best Friend*, which is kind of a joke because the boy is nowhere near ready to be a

mischievous

unselfish

man, except for a few times here and there when he actually thinks about other people first and makes an unselfish decision. But more often than not, the kid's your average goofy twelve-year-old and the dog is content just to hang out with him.

Matt's always liked a lot of action in my cartoons, so he keeps trying to get me to add explosions and runaway trains. I love that stuff too, but it doesn't belong in this comic. For *Man's Best Friend*, I want to show how much a pet can mean to a kid. I experiment with backgrounds, and my lettering is getting better. Dad thinks it's my best work yet but you can't really go by him.

I've been working on it all week, throwing away a zillion drafts that didn't work. I almost call it quits several times but remember something Umberto said about not giving up. The perseverance Umberto demonstrates in his cartoons—never mind day-to-day living—inspires me to keep going. It may take me a while, but I know I'll get there.

perseverance

I sit in the backyard against the fence with Bodi, underneath the wall of jasmine, and wonder if I'm a good enough cartoonist to get across how much growing up with him has meant to me. How excited I've always been to run into the house after school and see him waiting by the door, wagging his tail. How my earliest memory is putting my hand inside Bodi's soft mouth. How in half of my baby pictures, I'm lying on the rug alongside my dog. How he grabbed me by the diaper and pulled me out of the ocean when I was two years old. How he smells like summer after rolling around in the wet grass. How he always finds a little piece of sunshine to relax in, even when the backyard is filled with shade. How he didn't have any sibling rivalry when Frank came to live with us. How he always knows when to put his paw on the edge of my chair when I'm sad. How I never mind picking up his poop, even the two-baggers.

rivalry

Dad says a cartoonist's job is to try to capture moments in life that are funny or filled with real emotion. I doubt I'll be a good enough cartoonist to express all these memories in my drawings but I sure can try. I look over at my dog, grateful beyond words he's still alive. I reach for my marker and begin.

About the Author

Janet Tashjian is the author of many popular novels, including *My Life as a Book*, *My Life as a Stuntboy*, *Tru Confessions*, and the Larry series. She loves doing school visits and talking to kids about writing. She lives with her family in Los Angeles, California. janettashjian.com • mylifeasabook.com

author

About the Illustrator

Jake Tashjian is the illustrator of *My Life as a Book* and *My Life as a Stuntboy*. He has been drawing pictures of his vocabulary words on index cards since he was a kid and now has a stack taller than a house. When he's not drawing, he loves to surf, watch cartoons, and make his own movies.

illustrator